ENCYCLOPEDIA
OF A
LIFE IN RUSSIA

ALSO BY JOSÉ MANUEL PRIETO

Rex

Nocturnal Butterflies of the Russian Empire

ENCYCLOPEDIA
OF A
LIFE IN RUSSIA

José Manuel Prieto

Translated from the Spanish by Esther Allen

Black Cat
A paperback original imprint of Grove/Atlantic, Inc.
New York

Originally published in Spanish as *Enciclopedia de una vida en Rusia* by CONACULTA, Mexico, in 1998.

FIRST EDITION

Printed in the United States of America
Published simultaneously in Canada

ISBN-13: 978-0-8021-2077-9

Black Cat
A paperback original imprint of Grove/Atlantic, Inc.
841 Broadway
New York, NY 10003

Distributed by Publishers Group West
www.groveatlantic.com

13 14 15 16   10 9 8 7 6 5 4 3 2 1

For Elena and Alicia

La femme est le contraire du Dandy. Donc
elle doit faire horreur. La femme a faim, et
elle veut manger; soif, et elle veut boire . . .
Le beau mérite! La femme est naturelle,
c'est-à-dire abominable.

Woman is the dandy's opposite. Therefore
she must inspire horror. Woman is hungry and
wants to eat, thirsty and wants to drink . . .
Most admirable! Woman is natural,
that is, abominable.

—Baudelaire

Der Mensch sieht die Zeit nacht der Länge;
Gott sieht sie nach der Quere.

Men see time lengthwise;
God sees it crosswise.

—Martin Luther

ENCYCLOPEDIA
OF A
LIFE IN RUSSIA

ENCYCLOPEDIA. A porter offered to carry my luggage to the taxi stand. He awaited my response patiently, eyes glued to the floor. I noted the cloth cap, smoke weaving from a filter cigarette, the tight checked jacket, and in tones of *vox dei* delivered a severe warning from on high: "No rushing off to the taxi, boy. I've just arrived in P** and am not in the mood to go chasing after you. I'll bring you down with one shot or use a little gas—you'll be shedding some tears, believe me."

(That was me, barking orders like a ship's captain who must keep his boisterous crew in check, a skill indispensable to anyone who wishes to move about the Grand Duchy of Muscovy unscathed; without it I'd have little chance of bringing my ambitious undertaking to a happy conclusion, my luggage stolen right there in the train station by one of these fake porters.)

At the taxi stand I handed some bills to the unkempt individual in question, who made no secret of his disappointment. He swayed querulously on his short legs; it was clear he'd been hoping for a different sort of client. (He hadn't figured it out until he heard me threaten him with native fluency.)

"It's enough to buy cigarettes," I told him.

"Depends what kind. I'd like to smoke those . . ." (With an accusatory stare at the blondes he'd glimpsed in my pocket.)

I shrugged.

"Well," he said, "you would never carry other people's bags in a train station. Am I right?"

1

"That's true. I have other plans for my stay here in P**."

"Know something? I haven't always been a guy who carried suitcases around. A few years ago . . . Hey, be careful!" he shouted when he saw me open the taxi door.

I swiveled to gaze back at him, intrigued. He might turn out to be one of those insignificant characters we pay no attention to at the beginning of the movie, who then, two reels later, is revealed to be the murderer. Thank God it was only a bit of domestic advice he wanted to proffer: Be wary of taxi drivers, look both ways when crossing the street.

"Don't worry, it's not my first time in P**," I said, and once inside I rolled down the window and handed my pack of cigarettes out to the porter in distress: "Have a smoke on me, Dimitri!"

"(Kolia.)"

"Have a smoke, Kolia!" I repeated, then gave my orders to the driver: "The Astoria."

(Great floods periodically inundate Saint Petersburg. Sea swells from the Gulf of Finland rush through the mouth of the Neva River and wash across the lower parts of the city. Many buildings bear a watermark a meter and a half above ground.)

I. Listen: phrases that might at first seem simple, such as "Agreed, LINDA. At the end of the summer we'll take a trip to YALTA"[1] are merely cryptograms that enclose and conceal their true meaning, which is "Agreed, LINDA. At the end of the summer we'll take a trip to YALTA." This latter sentence composed, in its turn, of elementary roots, the primary concepts that are indispensible to any reader seeking to comprehend BREAD FOR THE MOUTH OF MY SOUL, the novel I'm planning to write.

I must set forth concepts such as KVAS, BOSCAGE (or FOREST, CO-NIFEROUS), INDIGO, in order to establish a framework of reference for the story I tell, a story that will exist in suspension among the vector convergence of these entries, or *voces* (voices) as they're known in my language. Set in small caps, to differentiate them, the entries are like black holes, exits into universes of other meanings, junctures crossing through the mass of the text to give it cohesion. Such a structure presupposes a reading that will be nonlinear and unending, for on consulting ROMANZAS you will be prompted to see RADIO, and that entry will send you to IMPERIUM, and so on interminably. Yet I do not seek a total sampling that would exhaust all possibilities; I'll limit myself to assembling a minimal number of entries that, in combination—Пропп (Propp) and his morphology of the folktale, Georges Polti's list of the thirty-six dramatic situations—can reproduce the Grand Duchy of Muscovy, the unknown world. I could have called this my *Expert System*, for mine is the type of ENCYCLOPEDIA that addresses a particular subject, works such as the *Enciclopedia Dantesca* or the *Encyclopedia of Modern Bodybuilding*, both of which I consulted in composing this opus. The simplicity of the subject matter, the overtly trivial idea of *frivolity*, of *tangential living*, diminishes the complexity of the method to some degree, even as it facilitates the task of keeping all the entries in mind. Moreover, the philosophy of the moment—which this ENCYCLOPEDIA seeks to summarize—operates by instants, exists in the present. The synchronic and circular conception of my work proposes the same thing.

It would have been easy to reorganize the text so that it advanced *chronologically*, much like Hesse's KLINGSOR'S LAST SUMMER, or any other novel written without artifice. But I deemed it more interesting for this reordering to occur in the reader's mind, as when, on turning the final page of a detective novel, all the pieces of the *puzzle*—the gloved murderer and that doctor in the first scene are one and the same!—fall into place.

3

Finally, a curious coincidence: in the *Instauratio Magna*, the ENCY-CLOPEDIA Sir Francis Bacon planned to write, the subject headings for the section titled "Man's Action on Nature" are almost identical to mine, it's rather extraordinary:

Vision and the Visual Arts. Hearing, Sound and Music. Smell, and Smells. Taste, and Tastes. Touch and Objects of Touch (including physical love). Pleasure and Pain. The Emotions. The Intellectual Faculties. Food, Drink, etc. The Care of the Person. Clothing, Architecture, Navigation. Printing, Books, Writing.

A few additional topics—EURASIA, HARD FROSTS, OPIUM—would complete the list for my project. (You already know the story: THE-LONIOUS arrives in Saint Petersburg in search of LINDA, the young woman he requires in order to carry out a delicate experiment. They are to make a trip together to YALTA, in the Crimea, and later, if all goes well, to Nice. The story takes place from late spring to early winter of 1991, months before the COLLAPSE OF THE IMPERIUM.)

A

ABACUS. The satisfaction of embarking upon this ENCYCLOPEDIA with an entry that figures on the first page of so many. We find the ABACUS throughout Russia. Fabricated of metal, wood, and bone. Displayed on many a counter as a guarantee of impartial computation, yet serving primarily as a means of swindling the buyer, who never quite manages to grasp, who follows the play of beads along wires, hypnotized. Having consulted the complex framework of the ABACUS, golden-haired oracles announce impenetrable results, weighted in their favor by at least 10 percent. (I've known shrewd customers to carry a pocket ABACUS for rapid verification.)

I often asked K** to teach me how to use one, an art she's known from the time she was a girl, but I never managed to get past the hundreds column to the final wire.

AGLAIA AND MISHKIN. I decided to follow the flautist: the group leaving the Kazan Cathedral's colonnade and setting out across the Nevsky Prospekt. The redheaded girl with a long overcoat thrown across her shoulders and two insignificant young men, trying to take her hand right there in full view, the rashness of youth.

As if they were valence electrons floating past a nucleus, ready to enter into reaction, THELONIOUS, who has some rudimentary knowledge of chemistry, maintains his distance from the trio, careful to keep his pulsating molecular mass out of sight. He watches them proceed along the bank of the canal and disappear into one of Saint Petersburg's extraordinarily beautiful gardens. When he reaches it, his fingertip reflects on the tall gate's Art Nouveau spirals, and he spies on them, wrought-iron flowers sketched in the foreground. He sees the girl sitting on a bench next to a tennis court. A great stroke of luck, for THELONI-OUS has spent hours studying tennis players in their animal innocence.

I. I stood there a while, watching the girl brush her hair. With every stroke, she swept it back from her forehead so as not to lose herself within it. I edged along the expanse of grass and sat down beside her (no one else on that bench, recently painted a deep green). When she had completed her *toilette*, the girl suddenly tossed her head forward and the hair flew, brushing against my face (its scent). I managed to catch hold of a lock and held it before my eyes in wonder.

The girl gave a start from behind her red curtain and her eyes, partly concealed in the ochre penumbra, clearly informed me: "I do not speak to strangers in parks." (And yes, strict Muscovite etiquette does prohibit such a thing, though in reality no one minds forming a friendship in the metro or in a department store, though never without alluding to the exceptional nature of the case.) Still, she ran her index finger from the roots to the ends to show me the uniform color.

"Forgive me," I said. "I wished to ascertain something. Many women use henna and manage to achieve rather credible color by that means. I needed a closer look."

"Come on! I can always tell when the color's natural" (at last she spoke to me). "Just look at the roots."

"Take this, please," I held out my card: THELONIOUS MONK. "I work for a company with an interest in natural redheads. We're planning to open a branch here in Saint Petersburg. May I—just one more time? Yes, I believe this is what we're looking for."

"*Cosmetics?*" the girl asked concisely, already thinking in English, too.

I hesitated. This way led to a dead end: boring sessions in the lab, diligent performance as a guinea pig.

"Please don't lie to me," she interrupted. I'd watched her lose her breath a while ago, in the cathedral. I had no doubt that she'd come with me, as in the end she did.

"Действительно, не знаю о чем это вы!" I answered, in a nineteenth-century Russian well suited to that garden. ("Indeed, Madam, I know not what you may be alluding to!") "It's the simple truth: we're looking for Slavic faces: high cheekbones, rounded noses. But it's your hair that interests us most."

"Oh, God! You're lying! I know it! Tell me more."

I wavered a moment and she stood up, ready to walk away.

"Sorry, I've got to go." She opened her purse and extracted a black velvet ribbon to tie back her hair.

"Look: I saw a book just now, in your bag. I knew you'd understand my proposal . . . And the black ribbon, it's lovely . . ."

One of the boys, the overcoat's owner, was returning to the bench holding two ice creams. Seeing me talking to his lady friend, he managed, with some effort, to articulate: "Nastia, you left my overcoat over there!" (Meaning: my friendship, my love for you. Me, who brings you ice cream!)

"No, I didn't; I was watching it from here."

LINDA's real name was Anastasia. I realized this at once, even as I realized that Anastasia was LINDA, but her friend's sad eyes troubled me. I explained this to the girl in a low voice. She asked me in English, *"I tell him go way?"*

I shrugged. LINDA took his arm and steered him away from the bench. They whispered energetically. Finally she ordered him to leave with a strong push, delivering it as if she were a forward for the Dynamo Moscow team. I've seen many Russian women do this. She went rigid, stepped back two body widths and shoved all fifty-five kilos of herself toward him. The boy lost his balance without taking his eyes from hers. He formulated a terrible insult—"Whore for tourists!"— and took off across the lawn, fast. This was certainly not, for example, the early-morning exchange between AGLAIA AND MISHKIN, the idiot prince, on the little green bench. But neither was it bad, for starters.

AGRICULTURE (*as practiced in* VILLAGES). The trees are so richly fragrant in the VILLAGE, and not in some distant past either, but right now. Like Anglo-Saxon America, the Grand Duchy is a great nation of immigrants. But these people have exchanged their Arcadias for a big-city Hades where they never should have ventured. The little clerk, who last night in his dreams drank full-cream milk fresh from the cow, knots his tie this morning with somnambulant fingers and it comes out far too short: a stubby Roman sword dangling over his round belly.

Muzhiks from Ryazan, hunters from the taiga, nomadic Kalmyks from Mongolia, all flung into the city's deep pit. Thousands, millions have fallen here, around the young gentry on their promenade, amid urchins who shout to their rustic friends: "Hey there! You! VILLAGER."

Since Russia is a country where nothing grows during the harsh half-year of winter, the eternal, obligatory question asked of the foreigner is: что у вас растет? (What grows in your country? You're not expecting famine this year? *Et cetera*.) Being from the tropics, where everything flourishes so exuberantly and we don't have HARD FROSTS, I would have to reply, "Millet, rye, artichokes, peas; raspberries in summertime, mushrooms in the fall."

AQUA VITAE. I reached out my hand, fingers fanned wide to indicate that I wished to see her ring. (I was losing momentum every second; the simple gesture of raising my elbow and extending my arm had cost me time, my hand creeping between the plates of salad to reach hers, adorned with the hypnotic stone.) Once aware of my interest, she stopped fluttering her right hand and offered it to me for a long moment of inspection. Then, seeing I was not content with simply admiring the ring on her finger, she took it off and handed it over with a smile, her ten red-enameled nails again describing a sphere, a wonder, the enormity of something.

The ring fit perfectly onto my fourth finger—the gold, the blue stone. Calmer now, I relaxed and settled back in my chair, gazing at her openly. I'd heard she was called M** and I had her ring. In under a minute, she'd stopped swaying between us like a pendulum and had shot me a look of conciliation for the man in gray at her left. But the man in gray was my new friend, wasn't he? I poured more AQUA VITAE—more vodka—for him and we clinked glasses. Suddenly animated, I sat up straight to propose a toast to friendship—my chin raised high—and, like a maladroit harlequin, under the poor cover of my own sleeve, gave the woman between us an energetic wink, a wink everyone saw—but what did that matter to me? *Et cetera.*

I caught up with her in the vestibule and she turned to meet me. She was wearing a knit dress with a high neckline, a delicate golden cross dangling low on her chest. I pulled her to me but lost her mouth halfway there, my teeth colliding with another blue stone near her neck, the softness of an earlobe. I perceived clearly that her lips (propelled by the same impetus onto my cheek) were parted and a voice—hers, but much more serious—begged me twice: "На улицу, на улицу!" (Let's go outside!)

Onto the dry snow that crunched underfoot like sand. In the woodshed, she opened her coat and without a second's hesitation we began paddling strenuously like two sailors swept by a powerful gust off the deck and into dark, cold water.

Who had given her the ring that turned loosely around her finger? In what strange language was she whispering so urgently? What was that intoxicating scent on her skin?

Ax (see: HAND AX).

B

Babionki (*бабионки*). There are, of course, women—or *mujeres* as I might prefer to call them—in Muscovy, but there are BABIONKI, as well, and these latter are superior. They wear their hair in a tight bun at the back of the neck and can generally be found in the bazaars, haggling at the top of their lungs, arms akimbo, over the price of a kilo of figs. They are very sweet albeit somewhat hardened by life in the IMPERIUM. Not every woman, I hasten to clarify, is worthy of the title. Both nerve and temperament are prerequisite. BABIONKI are much more commonly found among women of the people, though a number of female intellectuals, slightly derailed by the novels of Françoise Sagan, are also BABIONKI, as if consubstantially. When, upon arriving at a rendezvous in fine spirits and with every intention of sailing carefree through an inconsequential romantic interlude (our erudite commentary on Aubrey Beardsley at the ready), we discern, behind an elegant pair of glasses, the glint of a pair of BABIONKI eyes, it is highly advisable to retract the hand—though it may be halfway on its journey toward the skirt—indefinitely postpone this particular siege, and slip down the back stairs, giving thanks to merciful God all the while for the warning.

As a biological entity (they give suck to their offspring, which is a highly irrational mode of conduct) the BABIONKI eluded the rigid state control exercised by the IMPERIUM. In consequence, they've been the victims of perfidious defamation campaigns. But the BABIONKI, as "free men," до одного места about that—which is to say, *les importa*

11

un rábano or, in other words, "they don't give a radish" (or a "fig" or a "good goddamn").

BADEN-BADEN. I wanted to visit the apartment not far from the Astoria that F.M. once rented, now a museum. My visit coincided with that of a group of high school students who were studying Преступление и наказание (*Crime and Punishment,* the only one of F.M.'s books that is required reading in the schools). They were there for a class outing that included: a) the itinerary of RASKOLNIKOV prior to his crime; b) the slum where the pawnbroker and her half-sister Lizaveta lived; c) Hay Square, and a tour of the writer's private world: whipped cream for breakfast, the (very ugly) stippled wallpaper in his study, the goose quill from which sprang the imaginary life of Dmitri Karamazov, the heavy oak desk—indirect cause of F.M.'s death ("he ruptured an aneurysm trying to move it," the guide informed us in a whisper)—the pendulum clock stopped forever at four a.m., January 28, 1881 . . .

A scant hour later I abandoned the museum feeling completely empty. It was always the same story. A few years earlier, I, too, had redone my room in a wallpaper that was frankly appalling. But I hadn't managed to extract anything from its infinitely repeated design, whereas F.M., as all of us know, did. How to explain such widely differing results for two writers who both proceeded from such essentially similar wallpaper?

I. Next to the coat check, on a counter, the twelve volumes of his complete works were on sale. I paused to leaf through a copy of the diaries in the vain hope of chancing upon some answer to my question. As I was preparing to depart, I was intercepted by a very neat elderly little man wearing a woolen vest of 1953 or 1957 vintage who clicked his heels in military fashion.

"Allow me. I see that your interest is real. When I encounter a visitor who is truly interested, I take the trouble . . . You can see . . ."—and he held out a binder with the following inscription, in gilded letters, on its cover: *Dostoyevsky, F. M., Dossier.* "To tell you the truth, no one commissioned this investigation, not officially, so to speak . . . But please, forgive me, may I invite you to . . . That is, if you happen to have the time, of course. Perfect. Not far from here, just around the corner, as they say. An ideal spot for discussing the matter."

We emerge onto the street. Just a slight movement of our shoulders allows us to go back twenty, fifty, a hundred years with no difficulty whatsoever: to break through the threshold's flimsy partition and cross cleanly over an entire historical period. (Heavy, thick, larval: a cannonball's blind trajectory.) We descend into a tavern on Vladimirskaya Ploshchad: warm beer and drunkards sprawled on the tables, off to a decidedly bad start on their day. We take over a table beneath a large barred window, our heads at street level. Hundreds of feet pass by interminably as we sit conversing below.

"I would like to make one thing clear from the beginning. What I'm going to tell you is not, to any degree, the product of my imagination. Fyodor Mikhaylovich spent four years in the Omsk prison camp, the ка́торга, I understand that well. The sinister influence, the indelible mark it left upon the young writer's soul . . . For when else did Dostoyevsky develop his scandalous affinity for games of chance: enormous sums of money wagered, hands still clutching the playing cards at dawn? A vice, please keep in mind, that in my day would have earned him a far lengthier prison sentence, or even расстрел, as you are surely aware."

(But of course! *Rasstrel,* the pretty word: the convict barefoot in the snow, the signal, the nine flashes of gunpowder!)

"Well then, my fine gentleman, after all these years, what is the result today? That this compulsive gambler, lover of roulette and all forms of gaming, has a museum devoted to him in Saint Petersburg, and three more across the Union. Just think of that! But better yet: listen to me, sir, judge for yourself to what point . . .

"'Dostoyevsky, F. M., born in Moscow on 30 December, 1825. From his earliest youth . . .' No, let's skip that part and go straight to page 20: 'During his first trip abroad, in 1853, already an adulterous spouse (María Dimitrieva, his first wife, lay dying in Tver), F.M. evinces an excessive affinity for gambling.' Listen to this: in BADEN-BADEN, his lover (Apollinaria Suslova, the Polina of Игрок, *The Gambler*) writes in her diary: 'F.M. plays roulette constantly and in general his conduct is far from responsible.' That very same night she adds, 'F.M. has lost a lot of money and is very worried. We are left without funds for the journey.' Can you imagine? Truly catastrophic. I shall go on: F.M. spends three days in BADEN-BADEN, from 21 to 24 August, 1863, gambling at the casino. He wins 5,000 francs, a fabulous sum for that era, which he loses the same night. That year he gambles in Wiesbaden and in Rome. Finally, after his return from Italy, he bankrupts himself entirely in Hamburg. A note in Miss Suslova's diary confirms it: 'Received letter from F.M. yesterday. He has lost all his money gambling and begs me to send him more funds. I have no money either. I just gave everything I had to Mme. Mir. I've resolved to pawn my watch and chain.'

"Shameful conduct! And can you believe that this report of mine has been circulated to various powerful entities with no result whatsoever! You cannot imagine the harm it does us, this worship of false idols. I saw those children, God's little angels, innocently, without anyone to warn them . . . Well, and the worst of it, what is truly horrendous . . ."

The old man leans toward me and descends to a whisper. "A true story: a case of child perversion in a bath house. A subject on which the greatest silence has been preserved but which, nevertheless, was a secret well-known to many in the eighties of the last century. Strajov, his most intimate friend . . ."

I cut him off. "Excuse me, I don't believe I have any interest in this."

"But it's true! The most important part of my report! Count Tolstoy certainly knew about it. To be perfectly honest, I myself . . . at times (for I am no saint). Certain slender twelve-year-old backs . . . Напрасно сударь, совершенно напрасно! (You are making a mistake and you'll regret it!)"

I couldn't believe my ears. "Certain supple, bare twelve-year-old backs . . . frail, honey-hued shoulders" (*Lolita*, Vladimir Vladimirovich Nabokov—or Набóков, if you like).

I stormed to my feet, head spinning, cheeks on fire. Barely keeping my balance, I headed for the exit. In the doorway, unable to restrain myself, I turned and shouted back at this Humbert: "But this is a vile slander, a filthy донóс! Clearer than water! Aren't you ashamed! And there I was, hearing you out without an inkling of your true intent! To defame the memory of a great writer thus! Listen . . . A viper, that's what you are. A viper who lurks waiting to inject others with your venom. How low can a man . . ." *Et cetera.*

BIBLIOSPHERE. We can imagine it as an immense spherical structure, Ptolemaically centered on every man-reader. Its thin walls—thick as a single page from the Bible—harbor all texts that have been written and all those being written at this moment (including this one), their surface ceaselessly expanding. The vastness of the BIBLIOSPHERE, its cosmic diameter, in no way slows the velocity of access to its texts, for any journey across it is mental and instantaneous. After a more or less exhaustive exploration of the BIBLIOSPHERE a writer who is less than shrewd may enter a perilous state of ecstatic dejection, having deduced that nothing new can be created. A dynamic intelligence—one we might qualify as Copernican—will understand that we must return to the scholastic practice of the gloss, acknowledging the BIBLIOSPHERE as an authority. All that remains then is to discover the generative nature of the BIBLIOSPHERE, its capacity to create texts out of itself. Bacon writes, in *The Masculine Birth of Time or Three Books on the Interpretation of Nature,* "A pig might print the letter *A* with its snout in the mud, but you would not on that account expect it to go on to compose a tragedy." The theorem of the British Museum proposes virtually the same thing: "If an army of monkeys were strumming on typewriters they might write all of the books in the British Museum" (Arthur Eddington, *The Nature of the Physical World*). Or, to simplify things a bit, the monkeys might limit themselves to the thirty-five volumes of the *Encyclopedia Britannica.* Indeed, why not suppose—again, Copernicanally—that literature is no longer the province of mankind, that the fictional corpus will henceforth emerge by spontaneous generation from the depths of the BIBLIOSPHERE: originality of style, exquisite composition, the stamp of genius all the results of a roll of the dice, or rather, an automated spin of the painstakingly labeled spheres of a combinatorial optimization machine.

BOGATYR (богатырь: *mythic warrior*). We might call him a colossus out of a medieval epic poem of heroic deeds. He represents the немереная (incomparable) force of the Russian nation. Many secretly know themselves to be BOGATYR, a conviction for which no evidence whatsoever is required. One need only sprawl next to the wood stove, drink KVAS, be large-bellied and wide-shouldered, and remain imperturbably in that reclining position until the fateful day arrives: the day when little Mother Russia is in need.

In everyday life, the term has been put to unfortunate use as the name of a chain of shops that deal in plus-size menswear.

BOOGIE SHOES. Now, as I stand before the Astoria's gilded logo, I must say a special word of thanks to VASARI, the Italian shoe manufacturer, who have provided me with an excellent pair of *my first alligator shoes* with reinforced soles. They are exceptionally comfortable; the foot "sleeps" within them. Ideal for undertaking my search for LINDA.

At moments of discouragement, I would come to a stop in the middle of the Nevsky Prospekt and contemplate my shoes from above: their perfection, the solid stitching along their seams, was confidence-inspiring, OCCIDENTAL. A weight would fall from my shoulders at such moments, I would breathe deeply and go on my way, more certain of my own talent, more convinced I would be able to bring my project to fruition as long as I was wearing these formidable shoes, so fully aligned with the stars, so perfectly calibrated to the zeitgeist, so delicately musical. (Yes, incredibly enough: this whole rich gamut of sensations.)

I. Mere contact with certain objects of a reality not abandoned to its free play but organized according to strictly hierarchical criteria of quality and class inculcated me with a strong notion of authenticity, of absolute worth, a mental alteration that, over time, redounded to the benefit of previous efforts to correct my careless ways.

I will illustrate this with an example. On one occasion I spent several days contemplating the purchase of two pairs of shoes, both made of genuine leather and both in the very latest style, but each in a different color: one gray, the other blue. Gray and blue! The possibility of buying them (I had the money), reinforced by the other and even more hallucinatory possibility of choosing between two pairs of new shoes, not at all flashy, magnificently well made, occupied my mind for a week. In the end I acquired neither pair, but I had enjoyed the pleasure of taking them, albeit abstractly, into my life's eccentric orbit, which, in the wake of that experience, came to revolve around truly notable things, things guaranteed by certificates of authenticity to belong to this new world that had taken so long—it was so far away and I was beyond the reach of its gravitational pull—to draw me toward it, but that, once I was beneath its influence—like those wandering comets that pass by the solar system only to remain confined forever within it—was a world I could never abandon, dazzled by the brilliance of its genuine elegance. Then, after that profound contemplation of the symbols of this new religion—the shoes resting on a velvet cushion, their little altar protected by a bell jar—and in full knowledge of what this step would mean for me, I began to make use of the fork, and my former affinity for eating with the knife alone, and far more rapidly than anyone else at the table, came to seem (and in fact is) a barbarity of which, inexplicably, I had previously remained unaware. I don't mean I'd never heard any criticism of the practice; only that I was incapable of acknowledging or attributing significance to it. The same thing happened with other innocent vices, less graphic ones that are more difficult to explain (such as the habit of urinating into the sink, which can be very convenient for those of average or above-average stature), which, when I finally became conscious of them, struck me as equally serious.

BOSCAGE (*or* FOREST, CONIFEROUS). We can lose our way in the FOREST. "Once, as children, we went into the FOREST for mushrooms and got lost. We shouted and shouted . . ." A person might wander for hours among identical trees without finding the way out, the moss on the tree trunk, the newly cut stump. Real wolves lurk there, heads thrown back in a howl, and that little hummock of bones is all that remains of an unfortunate passerby. There's the story of the little girl in the taiga who was killed by mosquitoes that sucked out her blood. People go into the FOREST in summertime to gather mushrooms and wild berries. Preparations for this journey are the same as those made

18

for excursions to the beach during my childhood: thermoses, insect repellent, and the soup tureen, a solemn ritual we must undertake with absolute seriousness.

"Russia has the greatest reserve of timber-yielding trees in the world . . ." We read this and other facts of much interest in the pages of *The Russian Forest,* a novel by Л. Леóнов [L. Leonov] that is as heavy as a wooden tenpin. In spring, immense rafts of logs are formed, which never reach their destination but sink to the bottom of the great rivers of Siberia. For Russia, too, is a consumer nation, but only of raw materials. This metaphysical consumerism does not require the laborious elaboration of bulky products or tiresome marketing campaigns, but merely the cutting down of countless hectares of virgin forest or the pumping of great quantities of petroleum, only to burn it off, just like that, without putting it to further use. If the ESTEPA (*or* STEPPE) represents the field of action, of deployment, the FOREST is where the Russian nation turns in times of danger.

The BOSCAGE is cold, dark, and silent, an aspect it lends to Russia itself, which, seen from afar, may resemble a "dark wood," *una selva oscura.*

BREAD FOR THE MOUTH OF MY SOUL (see: PANIS ORIS INTUS ANIMAE MEAE *or* P.O.A.).

BRILLIANT CORNERS. When he least expected it and in the least appropriate places, THELONIOUS would sometimes suffer a serious relapse of his malady. For example, the face of a woman with whom he was having an animated conversation would suddenly go flat, recede to an inaccessible distance and blur as if a ghost had passed in front of it. The image that a few moments earlier had been his talkative friend would first regress into an accumulation of features that still, for a second, preserved a vague familial resemblance to their owner, then come apart into a chaos of basic geometric figures. At that point, THELONIOUS would intuit that this was a woman's face; he would distinguish the clean outline of an oval (different from a circle because its perimeter is not equidistant from the center), two opalescent spheres (the eyes?) covered with a thin film (the eyelids?), the lashes (short, stiff hairs = bristles), the mouth, reducible to the figure of a broken ellipse. As if he were studying an X-ray, a purely geometric outline, the stroke of charcoal on canvas. Only then, as he went along losing points of contact, to be left wandering across immensities of blank plaster, immersed in a silence that was shattered, visually, by intense red flashes, sudden proximities, blooms of flame blindly spinning. Desperate, THELONIOUS tried to grasp hold of the two red half-moons that were patiently modulating words with secret urgency: he followed that vermilion flutter with apparent attention, aware that he was the person being addressed by this discourse that now, thousands of kilometers away, he could no longer grasp. With great care, fearful of losing his footing, he approached slowly, advancing along the narrow path of two rosy protuberances (almost certainly the cheeks), reordering this assortment of geometric figures that, evidently, formed part of his world, and that might plausibly be composed into a woman's face, seeking to determine the nature of that patch of red, now immobile in a pout of reproach. "But weren't you listening to me?" And since at that very moment he had discovered, finally, what it was (a pair of lips) and then immediately recognized their owner, the sound switched back on and with it, as if by magic, the meaning of the spiel she had just directed his way.

His malady was the product of a logical breakdown in the natural and involuntary gift of seeing. He was aware of the way we distinguish objects by the contrast between surface and background, the drop-off in light values around the edges, the intricate process of correlation required to endow the naked primary blocks that appear *at first sight* with meaning. He knew how, in slow evolution, those blocks acquire practical significance, the connotation of a known object: "a fireplace poker" and then not simply a poker but a magnificent poker, the patina on its bronze. In that sense, THELONIOUS found himself as distant from other humans as mankind is from the blackbird: the blackbird that has no history, not the slashed sleeves of a Renaissance tunic nor the voluptuous blooms of Jugendstil, or Art Nouveau. THELONIOUS could, at will, slip through the cracks of sight, descend into a total decomposition of the image, and then ascend back up to admirable syntheses, reaching a point where he saw the world as we will see it several centuries from now, for our way of seeing is also subject to an evolution and every era introduces changes into the world's appearance. Two years earlier, THELONIOUS had admired some watercolors by Dührer—Alpine vistas made during the painter's first journey to Italy—that, according to the caption, were the first landscapes in the history of European painting. Some of the sights THELONIOUS enjoyed after his terrible seizures might also have been the first glimpses of an art yet to be created. In the visions bestowed by his malady were present all of modern art's moves toward blankness, beginning with an entirely impressionist luminosity and passing through the coldness of cubism and the abstractionist aphasia to disappear into a polychrome whirlwind, entirely unforeseen. Except he'd lost control over his gift and let himself "see" in unexpected ways while remaining blind to simple sights, utilitarian visions. He would stop, entranced, before the irregular striping of a fold of satin, given over to the pleasure of studying it, endowing it with a meaning inaccessible to ordinary men. He would concentrate on things that might appear trivial but that meant everything to him: the beauty of a double row of buttons, the sunflower color of a friend's silk blouse, the slow curves of the chairs in a café . . . Then, overcome by an emotion that cannot be narrated—the true and absolute importance of those lines—he would fall, dragged down by vertigo and left blind, the world decomposed into tessellations, and he deep within them, groping for clarity, desperate.

But there was LINDA, to save him.

BRODIAGA (бродя́га: lit., wanderer). The garden beneath my window was like a scaled-down replica of the world I would one day resolve to venture into. I had only to abandon the blank page on my desk and go forth, advancing from tree to tree, my house receding into nothingness amid the birches. What was the breadth of this world? Immense: all Russia. The Volga, and Astrakhan on the Volga, and Samara, its fluvial docks with their barges of watermelons. Vast spaces overrun by the Russian soul; there one could dilute oneself without leaving a trace, lose all track of one's identity and earn kopecks enough for a meager dinner by unloading watermelons until nightfall, barefoot on that dock. I was not, in fact, Russian but I was well aware of the BRODIAGA life that several of its writers had led and though it wasn't the type of experience I believed to be important at the age of twenty-three, whenever I felt tempted to make a radical change in the course of my existence I entertained intense thoughts of the striped watermelons of Astrakhan.

To be a BRODIAGA is a state that separates us from the fragile edifice of the day's order, coffee at breakfast, a poorly remunerated job.

Quand tous mes rêves se seraient tournés en réalités, ils ne m'auraient pas suffi; j'aurais imaginé, rêvé, désiré encore. Je trouvais en moi un vide inexplicable que rien n'aurait pu remplir, un certain élancement du coeur vers une autre sorte de jouissance dont je n'avais pas d'idée et dont pourtant je sentais le besoin.

Which is to say: *If all my dreams had become realities, that wouldn't have been enough for me; I would have kept on dreaming, imagining, desiring. I found an inexplicable void within myself that nothing could have filled, a certain movement of the heart toward another type of satisfaction that I could not conceive of but for which I felt the need.* (Letter from Rousseau to Malesherbes, January 26, 1762)

At this point in our reflections, we're ready to throw ourselves into vagabonding, to *brodiazhnichat*. Naturally the world abounds in empty-headed BRODIAGA—and ordinary men—who don't interest us, but I've met several contemplative or скиталцы вробіауа and occasionally we'll see one of them being interviewed on TV. For the BRODIAGA has other eyes that enable him to see very deeply and discern the hard nut of existence. I've never gone beyond mere admiration of the garden's foliage, but the fear of madness is there and does not diminish: a perfectly sane person can end up a BRODIAGA. Lev Tolstoy took his first step at the age of eighty-two and, inevitably, at the very start of the long journey, died.

C

CALLIGRAPHY. One day during an essentially sterile summer a woman friend had the following note delivered to me: "Don't think for one moment that I'll bear a grudge for what you've done. I've forgotten it already and am off to my parents' house. I hope your anger will have passed by the time I come back. Many kisses from the one who loves you. T**"

At ten o'clock in the morning when I was still wondering whether to get up, meditating in my bed about how to waste the hours of that day, she'd already had time to do her morning jump-rope exercises, water the begonias on the balcony, put on her only summer dress—the one with red polka dots—and take a minute to write me that little note. How could a person capable of composing such a note be incapable of doing anything in the world? "Don't think for one moment that I'll bear a grudge for what you've done. I've forgotten it already and am off to my parents' house. I hope your anger will have passed by the time I come back. Many kisses from the one who loves you. T**"

Her CALLIGRAPHIC writing was a further demonstration of the ease of her movement through a universe as precise as a clockwork mechanism, blindly guided by discipline. This was the source of her unvarying good humor. I could never achieve such handwriting. T** was, even so, a fine, upstanding woman who had all the grace of her flowery capitals. Her note made me happy (I'd come to love her a great deal) and saddened me at the same time.

I went down to the garden.

"Know what? I always thought CALLIGRAPHY was an antiquated practice, from the days when my father was studying it by the Edward Johnston system and all around us were beautiful PACKARDS whose looping contours are like CALLIGRAPHY compared to today's cars, which look like printed block letters. To discover a thing like this"—and I showed my lady friend the little note from T**—"is highly disconcerting, believe me."

CATWALK (see: PASARELA).

CHOCOLATES (SWISS). At the neighboring table, a uniformed general was gallantly attending to his companion, a lady who, I later learned, had amassed a fortune administering a meat provisioning facility. I invited them to join us, that we might all be the merrier for it: Muscovite simplicity.

Within the first half hour they'd already given evidence of astonishing appetites: raw silk kimonos, solid silver flatware, DACHAS with cedar-lined bathrooms and heated swimming pools, hunting parties with packs of hounds and beaters preceding them across the terrain, their heedless way of chewing, their formidable drive—in forty-eight hours they could have been sunbathing in Portugal . . . Or so the general informed me.

"Think about that, young man"—delivering a slam of his fist to the table. "In forty-eight hours we could have been sunbathing in Portugal. With our tanks . . ."—he leaned toward me. "In the blink of an eye. Let's drink to that!"

"For Heaven's sake, calm down! Who remembers all that now?" the lady administrator, who bore herself with the aplomb of a duchess, reproached him.

"Who remembers? All of Europe! They trembled at the sight of me! An officer of the Red Army!"

And he, meanwhile, had trembled at the wheel of a beautiful black sedan he had occasion to drive across a small European country, barely

on the map. The motor's muffled vibration, his officer's glands func-
tioning at full speed. He took the lady executive by the hand and cast
a dreamy gaze into her turquoise blue eyes: "That car was as good as
a Russian woman (wonderful, sturdy, well-built)."

a) Ready, in a word, to take up his position in the Archipelago contaminated by *evil*. When Russian troops laid siege to Berlin in 1945, Central
Command had already received several reports concerning a disturbing
Red drift toward the enemies' cushier digs: a petty predilection for trophy
watches that gave a fuller sense of time than the stubby Russian models.
Millions of soldiers who, at war's culmination, brought home the seeds
of movies not filmed in the Dovzhenko studios. It became necessary to
subject them to detoxification in the snowy fields of Siberia. (Remember
how RASKOLNIKOV comprehends the depths of his guilt as he watches the
blue sky through the tiny window of his cell in the Siberian prison camp?)

"Well, a car is a car," he added, to cover his broad back. He gave
me a sidelong glance. "I think the Lada won a stage of last year's
Paris-Dakar. What's more, our airplanes are among the best in the
world and at this very moment we have three men in the cosmos."
(Three men continually offering this salvation to the Russian people,
a last-gasp argument for faith in the nation.)

I was about to add something but we were distracted by the creak
of the swinging doors: RUDI with the CHOCOLATES. A beautiful box,
lilacs blooming across the lid. An assortment of bonbons.

"With liqueur?" queried the duchess, set on edge by this unexpected
apparition.

"An assortment," the writer explained, untying the satin ribbon.

The duchess, who at her many congresses and high-level meetings
must have dispatched more than a thousand such boxes, informed us,
"Of all the bonbons in the Union, my favorite are from Chelyabinsk."

Chelyabinsk? The city with a soccer team in the national league and a

uranium-enrichment combine? I spoke of SWISS CHOCOLATES but the duchess had been in Geneva and eaten her fill of them. The impression she had
retained was a negative one. "I'm not sure, perhaps it was too much milk;
very soft, as well. The finest CHOCOLATES are made here, in the Union."

LINDA passed the box around. The general, who, without yet actually having done so, was talking about throwing our rock crystal goblets
over our shoulders, selected a bonbon and plopped it into the executive's
champagne (he had heard that ladies like this), whereupon she grew stony-
faced, for the gesture struck her as being in dreadful taste. The general,
who'd anticipated a different reaction, shrank in his chair and made several
superfluous movements with his hands: he straightened his tie, the sort of
tie a VILLAGER would wear, pulled down the sleeves of his military jacket,
and twiddled his enormous cuff links, made of gold. His life was an endless thicket of false steps and it was clear that at this moment he hated the
lady executive, whose disapproval of anything she found in poor taste
was without appeal. She must have learned her manners at Party meetings, for she also severely reprimanded the general for crossing his knife
and fork over the plate instead of setting them down in parallel: that trifle.
She conveyed this to him in a brief pantomime, like a space ship captain
under zero gravity conditions, lightly picking up the offending flatware
and replacing them on the plate in the correct manner. Then she told him
in a whisper everyone could hear, "Do you understand? I will not even
mention the bonbon in the champagne. I'm not one of the sluts you soften
up with chocolate bars then take back to the barracks."

Her aplomb somewhat restored, the executive picked up the box
of bonbons and studied its provenance. "Greek bonbons? I've never
heard of Greek bonbons," and she bit into a particularly delicious
kind (which I'd already tried), filled with strawberry liqueur, and lied.
"They're quite bad, too. You should have ordered the chocolates from
Ufa; those are very good."

LINDA, who was also turning out to be rather an expert on CHOCO-
LATE, added: "That's because those other countries add too much milk;
in the OCCIDENT they try to save on everything. The Union's CHOCO-
LATES are purer. Unfortunately, they're hard to find these days; we no
longer have an adequate supply of cacao . . ."

The executive agreed with this, and explained, to my astonishment
(I, who'd taken it for granted that the IMPERIUM possessed the world's
most extensive cacao plantations), "We're not importing it from Brazil
because of the trade gap."

COLLAPSE OF THE IMPERIUM. As a uniquely privileged witness, the
manservant hidden in the stables who recognizes the trembling emperor—
despite the matronly cosmetics used to disguise his face—and watches
him saddle the thoroughbred for his flight, I, who came from territories
beyond the sea, watched the beggars proliferating in the metro stations
and discovered—my heart in my throat—purple graffiti that denounced
the cruelty of the IMPERIUM, all the spilled Russian blood. I saw my own
years of savings devoured by runaway inflation; I dined for three dinars
one evening and breakfasted the next morning for a thousand. I learned
to live without the security, the hope, the center of the universe that was
the Doctrine, and every day awoke with a smaller portion of soul, seeing
more clearly, yes, but diminished ever further by the awareness of my error,
the years gone by in vain, all that I had wagered on a false emperor. I was
attacked in my own home by men sent from the Sassanid Empire in search
of gold; I leapt into the void with my hands bound, like a Hindu prince
escaping from his alcazar as it crashes down in flames around him, then
fleeing at full gallop, hugging the neck of his steed. And my despair was
such that I was tempted to traffic in weapons for the IMPERIUM's southern
wars and I dealt in the electron, the yellow stone, provided to me by two
blond and insolent merchants from the Baltic.

I watched the IMPERIUM fall, saw its soul depart from its body through a thousand tiny cracks, saw that immense, enraged, and fearsome body emit wheezes of impotence until it collapsed, inert, abhorred, a shapeless sprawl on the ground, the occasion for photographs taken by tourists playing the triumphal hunter: one foot on the bear's prone mass, fingers in a V.

CONTEMPLATION OF THE IMPURE. *The naked body horrifies the aesthete.* This garret was undoubtedly ideal for P.O.A., the orphaned lightbulb high above, the translucent washbasin, the creaking floorboards. I lowered LINDA onto a brass bed next to the window. The girl, at last feeling the effects of the considerable quantity of champagne she had drunk, went on talking as if in a dream, enumerating the reasons for her negative response (but by now incapable of actually changing anything). I looked out the window, scrutinizing the wet ribbon of the canal and a few seagulls wheeling across the gray sky. I leaned out over the ledge a little farther. Yes: the bridge with the winged lions² was visible from here and I could mention it in my novel.

I loosened the buckles on her ankle boots and managed to get each one off with a single tug. I sat her up and tried to straighten her torso but her head swayed weakly on her limp neck. I raised her arms and pulled off the dress. When I had her in my hands at last, LINDA fell backward. Her inner framework, the ribbed structure that gave volume to her body's core, was now visible. Lamentably, she was only a woman. A naked body crossing through space in a bra and pink panties. I sat down in front of her and devoted one long hour to the study of her feet, the pink folds in their soles. How could such prettiness include these rough cracks, these calloused stumps? In despair, I moved on to the legs where I breathed easier—a nice roundness to the knees—and then continued slowly upward, her perfect figure installing itself smoothly in my memory, fitting itself into the emptied ideal of LINDA EVANGELISTA. In the distance her breasts began, the deep anatomical recesses, the dazzling whiteness of her neck, the red swirl of hair on the pillow. I cannot endure the sight of a naked woman for very long: no one can. That's why we always elude this moment, submerged in the shadows of close proximity, the single, blind, tactile continuum that is all women, the same basal heat. I subjected her (subjected myself) to this scrutiny because I sought to destroy any feeling of love that might otherwise contaminate the purity of my experiment. I examined her slowly, through the wee hours of that morning, piece by piece: the ceaseless play of valves, the measured flow of secretions, the unending skin like the surface of a Klein bottle, without a single point of rupture, artificiality, anything modeled by the hand of man.

It was getting lighter by the moment. A fly buzzed around and flew into the windowpane. LINDA turned over and I stood up in alarm. The black dot of the fly alit next to the girl's neck. I fixed my eyes on the distended skin of the twin beanies that were her breasts and as I approached to observe them better—those purple nubbins, the serosities beneath the skin—I retched and was momentarily overcome with vertigo. I wobbled back on my heels unable to tear my eyes away, irresistibly attracted by one of those pores, and realized in horror that I was falling toward it in trigonometric increments. Then I passed through the black hole and opened my eyes onto a white clarity.

月の光と云うものは雪が積ったと同じに、いろイロのものを燐のような色で一様に塗り潰してしまうので、滋幹も最初の一刹那は、そこの地上に横たわっている妙な形をしたものノ正体が掴めなかったのであるが、瞳を凝らしているうちに、それが若い女の死骸の腐りたダれたものであることが頷けて来た。若い女のものであることは、部分的に面影を残している四肢の肉づきや肌の色合いで分かったが、長い髪の毛は皮膚ぐるみ鬘のように頭骸から脱落し、顔は押し潰されたとも膨れ上がったとも見える一塊の肉のかたまりになり、腹部からは内蔵が流れ出して、一面に蛆がうごめいていた。

The moonlight covered the ground like snow, bathing all that surrounded him in phosphorescent splendor. At first he couldn't tell what sort of strange being lay there but after observing it a while he realized it was the putrefying corpse of a young woman. He knew the body had belonged to a woman because the skin and the extremities had kept their form and whiteness. But her long [red] hair had slipped off the skull like a wig and the face was a shapeless mass, swollen as if she'd been severely beaten. The entrails poked out of the belly and the worms were busying themselves across the entire body. (*Captain Shigemoto's Mother*, Junichiro Tanizaki)

I. Someone—a hand—helped me down the stairs. Once in the street, I collapsed to the pavement and dragged myself up against the wall like a BRODIAGA, filthy and in rags, resting after a long journey. I realized LINDA had left me there in the secret hope that I would never come back, that I would die, would forget her. I heard my own desperate panting as I tried to probe the distant walls of that deep black well and, little by little, my vision returned: sunflower seeds on the asphalt, a cigarette butt, still smoking. When the veil finally fell from my eyes, I saw, for the second time, the bridge with its Nubian lions, their gilded wings gleaming in the pale sun of the north.

With great difficulty I rose to my feet and crossed to the opposite sidewalk to take note of the building and the choppy curls of water in the canal. Suddenly, at the startling speed of a light source erupting into our field of vision, a Bach prelude flowed from one of the windows on the top floor. It was LINDA who, seeing me down there suffering in the light's unbearable brilliance, was making use of this simple and touching prelude to bring the chapter to a pious close. And—why not admit it?—I was overwhelmed with true emotion, standing in front of that gray building, with LINDA in her garret, and the flapping wing of a sob hit me full in the face.

Other sources: 1) *Cristo in scurto*, Andrea Mantegna, 1480; 2) *Danaë*, Gustav KLIMT, 1907.

CZARS (TWILIGHT OF THE). In a Saint Petersburg antique shop I discovered an old photo album and spent half an hour examining it in minute
detail. It opened with a postcard bearing an image in sharp focus of a
woman who, to judge by her dreamy air, had gone out shopping that
morning, more than seventy years earlier. An annotation on the back
was written in Roman characters, "Vera Vasilievna, 1907," and when I
had managed to decipher this, it left me pensive, uncertain of having
understood correctly. In the dead language of the first IMPERIUM, those
words may have meant something else, may have possessed a significance
different from the one we attribute them today. Clumsily translated into
modern Russian, they emerged, dragging along the blue-green algae of
a past that was hard to imagine. (How many Veras had I met, irrelevant,
insipid Veras, not one among them capable of carrying a parasol with
this woman's grace?) And the photo's Saint Petersburg was gleaming
and resplendent. Vera Vasilievna (I decided it was a woman's name, this
woman's name) had stopped at the edge of the sidewalk and a cross-
hatched sea of paving stones, gleaming like fish, opened out at her feet.
Their wet twinkle reflected the woman's white form, and since I happened to be in Russia (that narrow, poorly ventilated store, the vibration
of the tramway on the bridge, the red sun of the north) I thought of the
specular image of its Byzantine temples built next to lakes, and also, of
course, of the Grad Kitezh, the submerged city of Russian legend. (On
the banks of Lake B, the reflection's inverted temple, A1, seems more
real than Temple A, which rises in the air. If we listen closely we can
hear bells ringing, the sound dulled and condensed by the water's mass.
A *grad* where a perfectly coherent subaqueous life goes on: muzhiks
sharpening their knives in the marketplace, the assembly of boyars
[боярин] plotting the czar's death.)

The old Saint Petersburg, which had also sunk beneath the waters,
threw off faint sparks from the depths of that yellowing postcard: the

endless double row of buttons on V.V.'s dress, her starched collar, the fine lambskin of the gloves she clutched in one fist. Standing there on the edge of that sidewalk, V.V. had all the presence of an idol sculpted in metal, the full support of the strong wind that ruffled her bronze garments. The message transmitted by her figure was, nevertheless, one of petit bourgeois warmth, a life lived *frivolously*, and the picture could be broken down into the following primary elements, or rather was the point of vector convergence for the following weak forces: a) the Czar, who was perfectly cast in his role as the last monarch, an individual who disbelieved in the throne (the transition from His Imperial Majesty Nicholas II to simple Nikolay Alexandrovich Romanov seems to have caused little pain to the former Emperor of Russia and even afforded him more time to lavish the pages of his diary with mundane jottings); b) the triumphal apotheosis of Diaghalev's Ballets Russes in Paris, the black shadow of V.V.'s beautiful hat prefigured in Bakst's daring set design for *L'aprés-midi d'un faune,* which also derived its effects from great swaths of darkness; c) the sky blue background of *La Musique* and *La Danse,* the two great canvases by Matisse that adorned the mansion owned by the celebrated patron of the arts Sergei: Shchukin (that photo album also contained a picture of a male in his forties with abundant sideburns and an old portable Kodak in his hands, a vacant figure, devoid of any inscription on the back into which I could pour my concept of an eminent industrialist); d) the lovely Art Nouveau chalet Chekhov built in YALTA in 1899, to die there eight years later, and the equally wondrous edifice I discovered one afternoon while strolling along a Saint Petersburg canal; e) the following VERSES by Gumilev, the "decadent" poet who died before a firing squad in 1921:

Hay más tristeza hoy en tu mirada,
y son más tenues los brazos que ciñen tus rodillas.

Today the sadness in your eyes has grown,
And your arms, wrapped round your knees, are thinner.

Vera Vasilievna, or the woman in the photo, was very beautiful and for a moment I thought she might be Áнна Ахмáтова, Anna Andreyevna (Akhmatova) herself. What's more, an advertisement in the store window behind her featured a gigantic pencil that might be taken to suggest the woman's profession, her relationship to the world of letters. Couldn't the initials V.V., for Vera Vasilievna, be a key that we should invert to read A.A. (Anna Andreyevna), the specular image, the Grad Kitezh, the Saint Petersburg that lies beneath the waters?

Before leaving the store, I acquired a lovely lorgnette that Nabokov, in *Speak, Memory,* had given up for lost. (Says Nabokov: *That lorgnette I found afterward in the hands of Madame Bovary, and later Anna Karenin had it, and then it passed into the possession of Chekhov's Lady with the Lapdog and was lost by her on the pier at YALTA.*) But I found it there amid the jumble of history. There can be no doubt that by 1907—the year of the postcard—such lorgnettes were long out of style. This one might have had a place in V.V.'s parlor, displayed on the piano as an exotic touch. Such lorgnettes had the heft and presence of those old instruments of measure that allowed a very ample margin of error but—since they operated by the confrontation of analogous magnitudes—also granted a more intimate knowledge, one that cannot be achieved with a pair of these dehumanized modern glasses made of plastic.

D

DACHA (дáча). In 198* I lived for a long while in a small town, practically a VILLAGE, next to a wide river. In the afternoons, I would stroll down to its bank and, captivated by the grandeur of what was virtually an immense inland sea, would spend hours admiring the beauty of the landscape. Sometimes, for a long second, there appeared before me all the good books I would one day write: a precise vision of my future fragmented not into days but into the works that would someday appear under my name. What remained was the annoying task of writing them. (In the winter, a meter-thick layer of ice could support the weight of trucks loaded with wheat, and there, again, was I, observing the scene, amazed that they didn't plunge straight to the bottom of the river: truck, driver, and grain.)

To live there was like dwelling in a DACHA on the outskirts of some large city on the outskirts of the world. I knew that not far from Moscow a town of DACHAS had been built for writers loyal to the IMPERIUM, where they'd spend their summers, each and every one describing the flight of the selfsame grouse, the same rosy-fingered dawns. So strong was this custom of writing in DACHAS that, even when they became fugitives from the IMPERIUM and were declared to exist outside its laws, many writers took refuge—for what occult reason I know not—in DACHAS. The fearsome Solzhenitsyn completed his blood-curdling circumnavigation of the Archipelago in a DACHA that belonged to Rostropovich, the famous cellist. The beautiful Anna Akhmatova lived out the end of her days in something like a small DACHA, the "cabin

35

in Komarovo" which, according to her biographers, at last accorded her the peace of a home of her own. Finally, the entire Pleiades of the IMPERIUM's bad writers (such as Yevtushenko, Mijalkov, and a very bad one indeed, Bondarev) lived in DACHAS where, as if thereby constricted or encumbered, they slipped into a comfortable prose, the flight of the selfsame grouse, the same rosy-fingered dawns.

Perhaps private DACHAS still exist—it would appear that Alexander Isaievich (Solzhenitsyn) inhabits one in a Vermont BOSCAGE—but I maintain that the DACHA-IST era had a negative impact on Russian literature. (In self-justification, certain Pushkinists—all of them owners of DACHAS—paint Pushkin's retirement in Mikhailovskoe during the autumn of 1825, a period that can obviously be characterized as DACHA-IST, as a time of superproductivity. And therefore, if Pushkin himself . . . That is, given that we find traces of DACHA-ISM in this genius, too, *et cetera*.)

I, too, had my DACHA-IST period, and to be perfectly honest, I've never written more or better. I would get up every morning . . .

E

ESTEPA (степь, *or* STEPPE). Observed from the sky for a period that stretches across centuries, the color of the STEPPE vertiginously changes as it is traversed by myriad beings and overrun by shimmering waves of AGRICULTURE beneath the microscope that is the passage of the epochs. (You might also want to imagine raising a languid arm and placing the finger of Providence, the mark that designates the chosen one, on an obscure Mongol horseman, tautening his bow at full gallop, who, just as he's about to release the arrow, discovers in horror the Absolute Presence of God and topples over dead, flat on his back in the grass.)

The STEPPE is the low-pressure zone where the Golden Horde, the violent cyclone that uprooted the Kievan Rus, took on more water vapor and increased its wind speed. But when the Horde disintegrated into the shreds of impotent nomadic tribes, the Muscovite lava flowed toward its rarefied savannahs and little by little—a period of time measured out in centuries—reached the coasts of the ocean called Тихий (Tiji), an adjective that can be translated from the Russian as "pacific," or peaceful, calm, and smooth, but that also allows for translation as "peaceable," in the sense of nonwarlike.

I deduce, therefore, that it was a sensation of calm, of journey's end, that overtook the first explorer who sighted the edge of that other STEPPE, its vast blue immensity. An identical apathy is provoked by the real STEPPE, seen from the window of our train: it is interminable, empty, desolate, devoid of food.

EURASIA. In 1949, two scholars in Hamburg discovered the slow march of a glacier toward the Elbe. Some still cling to the erroneous notion that Europe extends to the Urals, but in fact it is Asia that extends to the borders of Western Europe. Russia, the IMPERIUM, is an Asiatic country, one that happens to be inhabited by pale-skinned peoples.

I. It seems fitting to amplify this entry with the following notice on the Hyperboreans offered by Gaius Plinius Secundus in his *Naturalis Historia*. In Book IV, paragraph 89, we read:

Pone eos montes ultraque Aquilonem gens felix, si credimus, quos Hyperboreos appellavere, annoso degit aevo, fabulosis celebrata miraculis. ibi creduntur esse cardines mundi extremique siderum ambitus semenstri luce solis adversi, non, ut imperiti dixere, ab aequinoctio verno in autumnum: semel in anno solstitio oriuntur iis soles brumaque semel occidunt. regio aprica, felici temperie, omni adflatu noxio carens. domus iis nemora lucique, et deorum cultus viritim gregatimque, discordia ignota et aegritudo omnis. mors non nisi satietate vitae epulatis delibutoque senio luxu e quadam rupe in mare salientibus; hoc genus sepulturae beatissimum.

Behind these mountains and beyond the north wind there dwells (if we can believe it) a happy race of people called the Hyperboreans, who live to extreme old age and are famous for legendary marvels. Here are believed to be the hinges on which the firmament turns and the extreme limits of the revolutions of the stars, with six months' daylight and a single day of the sun in retirement, not as the ignorant have said, from the spring equinox till autumn: for these people the sun rises once in the year, at midsummer, and sets once, at midwinter. It is a genial region, with a delightful climate and exempt from every harmful blast. The homes of the natives are the woods and groves;

they worship the gods severally and in congregations; all discord and all sorrow is unknown. Death comes to them only when, owing to satiety of life, after holding a banquet and anointing their old age with luxury, they leap from a certain rock into the sea: this mode of burial is the most blissful. (Trans. H. Rackham)

EXPECTORATION (*OR* SPITTING). The Muscovites are exceedingly adept EXPECTORATORS. They constantly announce плевать мне на все (I spit on this and on that), and at the appropriate point in the diatribe emit a *ptui* of profound disdain that is the impeccable acoustic counterpart of SPITTING. Despite what might generally be supposed, this pantomime is not frowned upon; everyone does it and it is quite theatrical. But a real EXPECTORATION—so innocent a thing, a simple gob of saliva on the lawn—sends them into near-hysterics; first because of the lawn (they are great lovers of *verdure*), and then because it's so very "ugly." And the false but sonorous *ptui* is not? What do you make of this, K**? And of the way they crack sunflower seeds in public and toss the shells to the ground?

F

FLUTE (MAGIC). The decor of the fall of the IMPERIUM included street musicians, felt hats at their feet anticipating the occasional crumpled ruble or some small change. MONK was taken by surprise as he shot beams from his eyes to probe a Byzantine church's multicolored cupolas at the far end of the canal for, at that very moment, the high notes of a FLUTE made him turn his head.

I. I panned rapidly over the bear cub exhibited in chains so that cruel children could be photographed with him, the Great Man on his pedestal, the stone fountain. Another warble from the flute. I finally located the musician who was clearly playing for his own delight, far from the public. I would leave him some money: for Bach, for the instrument's sweet tones in the lower registers, for the excellent acoustics in the chosen spot. You see, at first I took this musician for a boy (there was another boy nearby, a Cossack's overcoat on his shoulders), wearing a pair of jeans with holes at the knees and a long sweater. I understood my mistake when she raised her head to attack the next phrase.

I followed the melody with eyes closed, the original version of a tune I also knew in an adulterated rendition by the Swinger Singers.

II. A few months after finding myself surrounded by snow, when the imminence of nuclear war still troubled me more, much more, than the idea of giving K** a kiss, a friend gave me a recording of a group of Budapest virtuosi (FLUTE, clarinet, violin, and clavichord) playing Mozart. I had noted the name of that Austrian musician among the plans for "breaking through" I had sketched out during my last year of school, long before going to study in Muscovy, when I was still a model student, extremely conscientious in my fulfillment of what was expected and not yet gone to hell in a handbasket . . . politically, that is, to finally say it outright.

With all the gravity of one embarking upon a rite of initiation, I drew the curtains in my room to create a penumbra that would be conducive to my listening. The first chords sounded. I followed the violin's arabesques and the phrasing of the clarinet and before the end of the first movement was already fed up, unpleasantly surprised and disgusted by such irresponsible lightheartedness. The idea of *frivolity*, this ENCYCLOPEDIA's central concept, had not yet been installed with all its nuances and implications in my mind, but the ensemble of sensations Mozart's music aroused in me that day could only have been summed up by an allusion to *frivolity* in its most pejorative sense.

Preoccupied, I compared his music to Bach's—which I knew better —and the latter came out far ahead for the weightiness of his themes, the monumentalism, the seriousness of his proximity to God. Years would go by before I, happy to be young, without a speck of dust on my conscience, would enjoy myself while listening to the "jewel tones" of Mozart's music, a music that could justify my shameful inclination toward (SWISS) CHOCOLATES and Dutch cheese.

Bach and Mozart are names that may be impressive to some, but those who know what I'm talking about will not place the authenticity of this episode in doubt. For someone as concerned with transcendence as my former "I" was, and as my current internal "I" continues to be, Bach represents the fundamental framework of my musical appreciation, a phase that cannot be left behind, and as such continues to occupy the same place in my esteem. Only now, over him, or rather, surrounding him concentrically, Mozart has covered that primary skeleton with new and pink flesh, and today when I hear the works of the

German *Konzertmeister* I can readily discern the voids Mozart would later fill, the places where he would lighten the weight of the phrase to make it fly. Another aspect, no less important, is that in Bach no priority is given to the feeling of *lieder,* which the Austrian's melodies convey. Perhaps the fact that the latter wrote fashionable operas plays a role in this, I don't know. But Mozart's melodies have all the charm and ease of a song. This is something that the Russian Чайковский (Tchaikovsky) learned better than anyone else from Mozart. In this, and insofar as timbre is concerned, my quasi-compatriot Pyotr Ilyich and the Austrian Amadeus seem to me to be akin, both equally *beloved by God.* As product of an era when the once minor genre of the song has displaced all others, I am perforce most grateful to these two splendid musicians for their happy union, so gratifying to my ears, of the trivial and the sublime.

III. (Trapped within networks of reflections such as these, his vision enmeshed by that melody, MONK was henceforth prepared to see only LINDAS who were haloed by that celestial music.)

FLUORIDE. It took me years to ascend from the abyss of dreams into the superior levels of wakefulness. Before that, in the depths of my existence as a multipod amoeba, I had no ears for the death rattle of the cetaceans in bloody struggle against the flesh-eating orcas. I did not know that one or more public personalities had launched a proclamation that denounced my abyssal existence, I had no eyes for the gradations of the color blue and was incapable of distinguishing, among all the many oceans, the good one of free will.

But after my visit to the (CHINESE) PALACE, I developed a new organ to help me navigate the clean, clear waters of a full life. I acquired a vision that could reveal in sharp focus the secret components of that state of freedom. Something like the heightened perceptions of the hypochondriac who every morning lends an anguished ear to the arrhythmic beating of his own heart and discovers a new ache, a persistent sharp pain in the side . . . Still half asleep and in a bad mood, I jumped out of bed into an uncertain future in 198*. I went into the bathroom, chewed mechanically on the toothbrush, and was shaken by a sign of jubilation that shot through my nervous centers at lightning speed. My God! It was that magnificent toothpaste I'd bought the day before. I felt better and more confident, my mouth overflowing with foam. I stared straight into my own eyes in the mirror.

Spacodent was the name of one of those FLUORIDATED toothpastes.

I. *Frivolity* attacked the carbonic chains of the IMPERIUM with all the force reduction of FLUORIDE. The IMPERIUM, which had projected its considerable plantigrade weight into the distance of a perfect future, collapsed under the pressure of purebred dogs, the once impossible dream of Jaguar convertibles and soft Persian carpets, undermined by the new goal of a pleasant way of life that, over time, had managed to replace all its celestial objectives. It had been at least five years since anyone wore one of those awful striped neckties. That is: a profound antagonism had become apparent between the quietism of the Doctrine and the dizzying scandal of disposable diapers: between the search for a future kingdom of truth on this earth and the "general line" of the century, which was to consume the present and consider the future no more than a mental construct. The peoples held captive by the IMPERIUM peered out into the dark night, afloat on a warm sea awash in delightful detritus, to watch the illuminated ship that was the permanent carnival of the OCCIDENT coming toward them, and they heaved a collective, pensive sigh. "Yes, it's in a state of decay, no doubt, but how good it smells!"

THELONIOUS: To believe that the IMPERIUM fell for purely economic reasons is to commit the sin of pedestrian materialism and ignore the teachings of Weber. I've meditated at length on the phenomenon of *hits* on the RADIO. For anyone not in on the secret, it turns out to be very difficult to assay the strength of a *hit,* its devastating effects. A song that is trivial—or musically impoverished, which amounts to the same thing—can come to have greater social resonance than a manifesto, but this influence is surreptitious, masked. The effect on the Doctrine is that of a stealth bomb that imperceptibly changes mentalities, distorting or adulterating our ineluctable responsibility to do something, become something, be useful. The influence of the *hit* is called "ideological deviation" or "ideological penetration." A very apt name, for in reality what occurs is a kind of invasion by osmosis of the minds of people who want only to love, suffer, be successful, and live comfortably in a well-defined present moment between a yesterday and a tomorrow.

You might say there's no reason why this should enter into any sort of contradiction with the Doctrine of the Distant Morrow. Nevertheless, the latter ideology is predicated on a kind of asceticism, a life whose every sphere is political, which, in the final analysis, does not deny the earthly delights (which are even encouraged, very timidly, by its ideologues) but places a single great objective ahead of them. Two or three *hits,* the latest style, the irresponsibility of youth, enter into open conflict with these postulates (giving rise to the so-called "ideological struggle"). Youth, breezy afternoons, a generous portion of some delicious frozen concoction (VANILLA ICE cream, for example), demand a here and now that is thrilling, exultant, danceable.

FOREST, CONIFEROUS (see: BOSCAGE).

G

GREAT GATSBY, THE. In the bottomless sea of the IMPERIUM's former capital, a few islets of prosperity had lowered their anchors: full-fledged OCCIDENTAL boutiques, red and fluorescent. In front of one such establishment a few curious passersby were pointing to dresses that were very lovely and very expensive (like the gowns of Catherine the Great in the Hermitage, also behind glass: crinolines whose taffeta silk was very old and very distant) and, good Lord, ties that cost $30, an entire month's salary at current exchange rates, knotted at the collar of shirts made of printed silk—the last cry that year—which also seemed very old because they belonged to an inaccessible present. It looked like the window of a cabinet of wonders, PETER's Kuntzkamera: a mammoth tusk exhibited alongside a magnificent electric dishwasher.

I hadn't told LINDA I planned to buy her a dress for that night's dinner. She thought we were only stopping to admire the display. (Oh, yes, she'd seen leggings like these once before—*lycra* they call it—in a mail-order catalog!)

LINDA wanted to try on a dress that was very beautiful and very expensive, just to see how she looked. It suited her marvelously.

"It suits you marvelously. Have I mentioned that we're having dinner at the Astoria tonight?"

At last LINDA understood the scope of my plan. She was speechless, then asked me uncertainly, "Do you think anyone might take it the wrong way, because I accepted your proposition so quickly? It's a novel, isn't it?"

"It's silk, the very latest style, and it suits you marvelously."

I. The doorman at the Astoria shot me a frosty look. It was his job to find young ladies for the guests' entertainment and he was annoyed at losing my business. As we crossed the lobby several men noticed the threadbare jeans worn by the beauty on my arm and the large prominently labeled bag that I carried, with our purchases inside, and thus were educated in how to win young lady friends for themselves. I followed LINDA along the carpeted hallway, entirely surrendering to the measured waltz of her hips, her backlit red hair.

In silence, LINDA studied the magnificent copies in oil, the 1905 furniture, the Art Nouveau chandelier dangling from the ceiling.

"Isn't all this far too expensive just for a novel?"

"I've told you: I have ample funds at my disposition. I've been saving up for a long time and thinking about a redheaded girl like you. Look, I'll show you the shirts I've bought, all made of silk. Or no, this will give you a better idea."

We went over to the table where my open *laptop* lay.

"This computer cost me a great deal, and then there's the SCANNER, too. You don't know what a SCANNER is? It's a device that allows you to introduce texts directly into your computer without having to key them in. Very convenient since I've brought along a whole library. I'll show you how it works. Could you get that book down for me? The one I was leafing through this morning? Look here."

Recovering himself in a minute he opened for us two hulking patent cabinets, which held his massed suits and dressing gowns and ties, and his shirts, piled like bricks in stacks a dozen high.

"I've got a man in England who buys me clothes. He sends over a selection of things at the beginning of each season: spring and fall."

He took out a pile of shirts and began throwing them, one by one, before us, shirts of sheer linen and thick silk and fine flannel, which lost their

folds as they fell and covered the table in many-colored disarray. While
we admired he brought more and the soft rich heap mounted higher—shirts
with stripes and scrolls and plaids in coral and apple-green and lavender
and faint orange, and monograms of Indian blue. Suddenly, with a strained
sound, Daisy bent her head into the shirts and began to cry stormily.

"They're such beautiful shirts," she sobbed, her voice muffled in the
thick folds. "It makes me sad because I've never seen such, such beautiful
shirts before."

"Impressive, isn't it?"

"It's a new technology."

"Yes, in a sense. You're right. What more can I show you?"

HAND **AX** (топóр). The leafy BOSCAGES of Moscow: VILLAGES and monasteries depicted in vertical perspective. Monks who penetrate this verdant grove and piece together the first Muscovite kingdom with blows of massive woodsman's axes and без единого гвоздя (without a single nail). We are accustomed to viewing the AX as a tool for woodcutters. In Russia, however, there is always a HAND AX within a radius of five meters, at arm's length; they're as common as bread knives. The AX represents brutality, the не обтесанные (rough-hewn) side of the Russian soul. RASKOLNIKOV kills the pawnbroker and Lizveta with an AX. We know from Gogol that during HARD FROSTS VILLAGE idiots left shreds of their tongues on its cold metal. It may strike us as rather uncomfortable (and in fact, is), but the good Russian who has resolved to take matters to their ultimate consequences brandishes one of these and strikes, with no fear of the effusion of blood. The AX, as we noted earlier, represents the irrational, an animal terror. A.A. expressed it perfectly:

> *Fear stirs among the things in my dark room,*
> *a ray of moonlight shatters on the blade of an AX.*

HAM (ХAM). Both a son of Noah and a blasphemous oath.

כב .אָהֳלֹה בְּתוֹךְ ,וַיִּתְגַּל ;וַיֵּשְׁךְּ ,הַיַּיִן-מִן וַיֵּשְׁתְּ כא .כָּרֶם ,וַיִּטַּע ;הָאֲדָמָה אִישׁ ,נֹחַ וַיָּחֶל כ

.בַּחוּץ ,אָחִיו-לִשְׁנֵי וַיַּגֵּד ;אָבִיו עֶרְוַת ,אֵת ,כְּנַעַן אֲבִי חָם ,וַיַּרְא

אֶת וַיְכַסּוּ ,אֲחֹרַנִּית וַיֵּלְכוּ ,שְׁנֵיהֶם שְׁכֶם-עַל וַיָּשִׂימוּ ,הַשִּׂמְלָה-אֶת וָיֶפֶת שֵׁם וַיִּקַּח כג
,וַיֵּדַע ;מִיֵּינוֹ ,נֹחַ וַיִּיקֶץ כד .רָאוּ לֹא ,אֲבִיהֶם וְעֶרְוַת ,אֲחֹרַנִּית ,וּפְנֵיהֶם ;אֲבִיהֶם עֶרְוַת
כו .לְאֶחָיו יִהְיֶה ,עֲבָדִים עֶבֶד ;עֲבָדִים אָרוּר ,וַיֹּאמֶר כה .הַקָּטֹן בְּנוֹ לוֹ עָשָׂה-אֲשֶׁר אֵת
וְיִשְׁכֹּן ,לְיֶפֶת אֱלֹהִים יַפְתְּ כז .לָמוֹ עֶבֶד ,כְנַעַן וִיהִי ;שֵׁם אֱלֹהֵי יְהֹוָה בָּרוּךְ ,וַיֹּאמֶר
.לָמוֹ עֶבֶד ,כְנַעַן וִיהִי ;שֵׁם-בְּאָהֳלֵי

*(And Noah began to be an husbandman, and he planted a vineyard: And
he drank of the wine, and was drunken; and he was uncovered within his
tent. And HAM, the father of Canaan, saw the nakedness of his father, and
told his two brethren without. Genesis 9: 20–22, King James Version.)*

In the Russian language, HAM is a self-sufficient word, a Hammer
of Hams. I once observed an incident in which an individual mud-
died the quiet stream of a retiree's pleasant stroll and the wronged
party turned, terrible and full of rage, and SPAT "HAM, HAM, HAM!"
over and over at the HAM, defining him, singularizing him, putting
the handcuffs on him, preparing him to be caged and subjected to
public derision.

When you go out into the street, you may at any moment witness the beginning of legendary HAM sessions. (THELONIOUS MONK
in New Orleans, the night he sent out for the only drum kit, had it
brought to him across the sleeping city.) Old men and young ladies
do not cease to whisper the accusatory apostrophe in a rage, hissing
it out left and right.

I. To behave rudely in Moscow is almost to show a kind of defer-
ence to the victim of the aggression; it is to allude to a human quality
that is out of the ordinary, a capacity for understanding that is distinct
and Christian. Someone has shouted at you, and he is the bad guy,
the HAM, but (and herein lies the great challenge) are you not able

to forgive him? And everyone, all well experienced in this particular spiritual gymnastics, forgives everyone else, mutually, for their terrible fits of rage.

In a café we summoned the waiter to ask for TEA and had to wait half an hour for him to appear. When he did, he was highly annoyed, for we had failed to grasp that his activity as a café waiter was purely a masquerade, a job he was performing only to remain in close proximity to some secret chamber of speculation. He took our order with the demeanor of a king mingling incognito with the commoners who discovers, to his displeasure, that in addition to wearing the apron and carrying the pencil behind the ear—both indispensible elements of the disguise—he must also run from kitchen to dining room, take down orders, and endure the complaints of the clientele. All his wrath fell upon us for we continued to insist that he bring us clean eating implements and thereby won for ourselves the black hatred of that waiter, the HAM.

HARD FROSTS. Covered in rime, the leafless trees, their branches sketched against a sky dense as sea water. Numb with cold, we moved in silence as if this were a bed of coral and we the mute school of fish interminably shooting to and fro.

I've been scuba diving at a depth of three meters and it was exactly like this; the ice crystals sparkling in the air are the spots of light that pierce through the water's mass to dapple the seabed covered in coral, which is what trees look like at 32 degrees below zero (centigrade).

I. "This morning when I went downstairs to shake out the carpets, I realized immediately that we must be very far below zero because my eyelashes grew heavy with a coating of ice. It happened in a single blink."

I've opted for this detail about the eyelashes to give you a precise idea of the cold. (The real India, a writer—Nabokov—tells us, reveals itself in the green mildew that blooms on a pair of shoes left outside for the night.) I was in the garden, beneath white trees, and had to melt the frost off my eyelashes with the heat of my fingers. I have no such personal detail with which to illustrate life in the freezing barracks (I was shaking out the rugs as an *exercise*, enjoying the iridescent swirl of ice crystals): the slavering pack of dogs that rip straight through your padded trousers or the sweet indifference of dying from cold and inanition, the unfathomable abyss of an undeserved prison sentence, the appalling discovery that there's been no mistake whatsoever, only the refined absurdity that is the total absence of any system, the pullulating chaos beneath an apparent order, the millions of dead and your single concrete death (a pair of boots covered in mildew).

II. At last, in 1991, we learned that Óсип Эми́льевич Мандельшта́м (Osip Emilyevich Mandelstam) died in February of 1937 and that his body was piled along with others in a shed, where it remained until spring. An entirely apolitical piece of data: a destiny.

HIPPOLYTE. Just as RUDI began serving the truffled salmon, a violent thunderstorm erupted. Heavy raindrops beat against the windows. I stood up, for I needed to collect the gusts of water and the hooded sky's varied hues of gray. LINDA began to give me the news, then broke off: "It's raining, as you see . . ."

I nodded. It was ten p.m. and still light outside. It was raining—I could see that perfectly well for myself—but what else was going on? She held her hand out and touched the tips of my fingers. Something was making her anxious.

"I hope you won't take this too badly. I'll be right back."

She shot through the door in a whirlwind. I glanced at RUDI, the chorus of this Greek tragedy against whom all our dialogue rebounded, but he didn't seem to know the source of LINDA's sudden disquiet either. Was it the rain? Did she have white clothes hung out to dry on a balcony?

Five minutes later she was back, pulling young Maarif along by the hand. "He was going to catch cold out in the rain," she said. My soul plunged to the bottom of my feet. He had been waiting for her the whole time in the plaza. He would wait there, kneeling on the pavement, hatless and shivering with cold. I repeated his name in a low voice, "Maarif," trying to find some explanation for his conduct. What was more, with a friend like that, LINDA was dangerous, capable of standing at the altar before an open Bible and then escaping in a sleigh pulled by fiery steeds through the driving snow and the wind's eternal ululation. Which would cut short my novel.

No, I had nothing against allowing Maarif to join our party. "RUDI, set another place for Maarif."

Maarif was wearing his Cossack overcoat, doing his bit for the awakening of the national consciousness. He hung it from a hook on the wall and I watched the water drip from it, the steam that rose from its folds.

LINDA wrote me a short letter about Maarif. "Maarif is a Persian name or something like that. But he's Russian. He's the one who explained all those terrible things to me, about the Elders of Zion . . ."

I raised my eyes and fixed them on this young man: the clear, exalted face of one who has been granted access to a unique truth. He remained silent through most of the meal. Just before midnight, he summoned RUDI and said, so that everyone else could hear: "Tell me when it's midnight."

RUDI answered somewhat abrasively, "That won't be necessary; we close at midnight, unless we're paid a supplementary fee." (RUDI addressed him like that out of annoyance at the tone of his order; he was very intelligent for a mere waiter, but Maarif was too young to understand that.)

Half an hour later RUDI went over to Maarif and whispered something. I consulted my watch. Maarif leapt to his feet, prepared to unmask me.

(The same scene in F.M.'s Идиот [*The Idiot*]: the young man who wants to settle accounts with the world and offer up the irrefutable proof of a vermilion stain on the tablecloth. This was what happened: HIPPOLYTE, his left hand holding the glass of champagne, had plunged his right hand into his coat pocket. Keller afterward declared that HIPPOLYTE had that same hand in his pocket earlier, as he was talking to Myshkin, whom he embraced with his left arm—which was, Keller said, what first awoke his suspicions. Be that as it may, some vague uneasiness made him run to HIPPOLYTE's side. But he was too late. He only just glimpsed an object shining in HIPPOLYTE's right hand and realized immediately that a small pocket pistol was pressed against the young man's temple.)

"Nastia!" Maarif shouted to LINDA to penetrate her consciousness, which was somewhat impaired by the champagne. "The terrible thing, the worst thing of all, is that this guy doesn't have a kopeck, he's an imposter, a PSEUDO DEMETRIUS."

The fearsome accusation. I wanted to cut his wings before he rose much higher.

"The terrible thing, the worst thing of all, is that I have a great deal of money indeed! And I'm ready to spend it all on LINDA!"

My reply took him by surprise. He stopped short (pebbles still rolling beneath his feet) and gulped for air. He went on. "Why should we believe you? I, too, could organize a feast like this one if I wished, but that's the thing: I don't want to."

I was wounded by his total incomprehension. I had confessed my plan to him—all that the reader now knows—in the belief that he would grasp my purpose. But he had heard me out with the smile of an experienced practitioner who prefers not to contradict a patient who is visibly mad. I let him carry on ("Why should we believe you?" *et cetera*).

"When I saw you this morning along the canal, near the cathedral, I knew you immediately for one of those pathetic foreigners who put on airs of grandeur. I met one who wanted to be called the King of Suomi. He talked about renting a Navy helicopter to show me Petersburg as the crow flies. He never kept his promise . . . In Helsinki there are at least three thousand plumber kings like this guy here. As long as we have foreigners eating and drinking in our restaurants, seducing our women, the Russian muzhik will never be able . . ." and Maarif SPAT, irate.

Then the general let off another slam of his fist on the table. All the plates and glasses jumped.

"I disapprove of these statements," he formulated, as if delivering a report to Central Command. "You have eaten and drunk at this table. How can you deny your friendship with Hussein?"

(Hussein, the Assyrian scribe. Who was me. More or less accurately. The general had christened me with a generic foreign name, in the sense that I was any old common-garden Ivan.)

"Ask Hussein to forgive you," he demanded.

Maarif, red with shame, took a moment for introspection and found himself replete with champagne and caviar consumed at my expense. Whereupon he promptly delivered himself of a second discourse, this one of repentance for all the countries the IMPERIUM had dragged into the abyss, my own included. Finally, no longer knowing how else to erase his guilt, he praised my Russian. "You speak Russian very well"—which meant I had managed to open the doors of the *Rus* and could leave behind the STEPPE, the nameless distances that belong to those who are mute (those who explain themselves in an unintelligible language, a language of mutes), the sea and the lands beyond the sea, and enter the chosen kingdom of world renewal. Slavophilia. Russian exceptionalism. The Russian Third Way. Maarif wanted to reduce that whole vast task to the salvation of LINDA's lone, imperiled soul.

I. Dinner was over. RUDI, who now took me for little less than a desert sheikh, bent down next to my ear, his aching hand clutching the lapel of his double-breasted jacket, his lips moist: "You should go south, to YALTA. A lot of casinos have opened there. The season has just begun."

I

IMPERIUM. Captives in the IMPERIUM, its prisoners felt nevertheless as if they were galloping in full freedom across unlimited space: men and women in their natural habitat with no barbed wire or alarm system in sight. The IMPERIUM was a parallel world, a self-sufficient universe that included its own "globetrotters," fully deserving of the title, who, even so, had never left it. The other world—the OCCIDENT, Africa, the Fiji Isles—seemed to belong to a past accessible only through books or films that appeared to emerge from nowhere. It was perceived as a far distant future or a remote history (a purely academic interest in the Sumerian maritime arts); in the present it was nonexistent.

I. In this partial analysis of the IMPERIUM, I shall focus on the following aspects:

a) *Destiny*
b) *Fear*
c) *Mortal danger*

a) *Destiny.* Russia, the great country that constituted the nucleus of the IMPERIUM, possesses a universal *destiny* that is the sum of all individual *destinies*. The topside or visible portion of this great *destiny*, this ineluctable Russian *destiny*, makes its way like an icebreaker through the frozen armor-plating of the years, leaving behind a jagged wake of truncated lives. The currents of this *destiny* come from very far and cross through the IMPERIUM's lives like fossilized radiation left over from the Big Bang. And these narrative threads, invisible and inescapable, are *destiny*. Everyone is crisscrossed by these lines of force, fate's ultrapowerful magnet, drawing them to their death. With room for small fluctuations, fruitlessly heroic efforts, *the world as will and representation*, and other such trivialities that bother us only when we're young, after which, tired of rowing against the shifting tides of *destiny*, we extend our arms in a cross and float painlessly.

Russia (or the IMPERIUM) is struggling against its *destiny*, but the shadow of this fatalism pursues it. Many historic dates can be adduced to confirm the certainty of its *predestination*. Hence there is no increase in human morality nor absolute progress, but only the infallible pincer lowered from the sky which, from among the panicked and fleeing multitude—unaware that the danger does not exist for them—selects the idiot seminarian, with his bangs and wire-rimmed glasses, for its appalling fulmination, without motive, without cause, without delivering any verdict.

Destiny makes use of blind executors of its will who, as such, merit our comprehension more than our contempt. Russia is an old country and there one breathes the frozen air of multiple histories that bear out this theory of *destiny*. They know it and that's enough. They go out into the snow barefoot to face the firing squad's nine spurts of flame: merely the means chosen by *destiny* to send a concise message of utmost importance.

b) *Fear*. I've jerked the strings of small *fears*—my cruel half-smile —without knowing I was being watched on high by the omnipresent pupil from which all the underlying fear irradiates, and I have felt vertigo when I raised my eyes and discovered that fact. Each person's performance as the petty tyrant of our own tiny realm is a necessary movement of the soul, a display, a rattling of chains. Whether we like it or not, an icy wind blows from the Hesperides, *inhumanly*. Like God himself, *fear* is given a name and endowed with the limbs and torso of a state institution; this *fear* accumulates in the multiple guises of jails, the secret police, ministerial directives—only a few of the many incarnations of its absolute being.

This latent terror binds every organic compound; it can be found in all of them just as oxygen is found in chains of carbon. You are *fear* and something else, anything else. And through this intermediary, the inhabitants of the IMPERIUM enter into reaction, they function, agitating their blind pod-limbs and secreting the hard coral efflorescences of the State, which are interlaced with *fear*.

Though *fear* cements the imposing fabric of the IMPERIUM, life under the dominion of this *fear* is ethereal and unreal. Мы живем, под собою не чуя страны. (*We live without feeling the country beneath our feet.* Mandelstam.) The man who has experienced the terror of hearing his own guilty name shouted out in a formation loses faith; his image in the mirror dissolves and he closes his eyes and listens in anguish to the thud of the hobnailed boots as they come to a halt before him. I've discovered once-beautiful souls deformed by the abyssal pressures of the IMPERIUM, the unfathomable sea where they live out their one-celled lives. Hence the HAM's violent tempests, the ravages of AQUA VITAE.

The divinity of *fear* gazes down upon the lamentable tableau of the IMPERIUM and smiles in satisfaction from its celestial box seat.

c) *Mortal danger.* The enthusiasm generated by the IMPERIUM shortly before its collapse was the nervous grin, the last dying hope of the hunted man who, corralled at the edge of the abyss and about to be devoured by the monster, sees it stop short in wonder over the flutter of a passing butterfly, a sight that attenuates the fury in its eyes and creases the blue skin of its formless snout into a *human* grimace. In the brief instant of the miracle, the prey has a moment to give thanks to God, reevaluate the monster's perversity ("No, you're not bad, it was the years of isolation, the terrible conditions, I knew the change would come, I had faith in you"), and sidestep the monster's charge. Once on safe ground, shielded by an overhang, the escapee shouts the truth to the monster and spends all necessary funds to capture it, so as never to have to put the goodness of its nature to the test again.

INDIGO (*the color*). Lying back on my deck chair, the red PACKARD parked only a few meters from an intensely blue sea, I devote myself to *studying* the golden glints in the air churned by the bronze thighs of women emerging from the water. Seeing them, I thought of a superb slogan for a brand of shampoo or conditioner: "*Mientras por competir con tu cabello, / oro bruñido al sol relumbra en vano . . .*" a line from Góngora that could have been put to excellent use by Vidal Sassoon, the celebrated California hairstylist: "A rival to your hair, the sun / flashes on burnished gold in vain . . ." The bathers were advancing with that special clumsiness of terra firma, SIRENS dragged to shore by the sea to exhibit their magnificent colors, their backs treated with vitamin-fortified creams, their taut bellies, visually centered by the dark point of the navel: ideal graphic statements for the great cover photos of the nineties which, dreamed up in distant international centers, reached every beach in the world with the mandatory force of a ministerial directive. For a second, I imagined an impossible collision between the motley decor of the beach before me and that same bathing resort at the beginning of the century, its sepia tones entirely incompatible with this pure indigo. The terror those beige ladies would feel if confronted by the color pale

TTE OF THESE VERY BLONDE GIRLS, ALL OF THEM FORMER KOMSOMOL MEMBERS, DELIVERING CARELESS KICKS TO BEACH BALLS THAT WERE VERY RED AND BLUE AND YELLOW. Full, vivid colors, straight out of a magazine printed on expensive coated stock; the metallic glitter, the fine film that overlay their human souls with the finish of an industrial product, the high sheen of an inanimate object that the hard gazes of certain fashion models seek to copy, the distant bearing, the contrived expression. Already we were being blinded by the first flashes of the *neon look* with its tremendous artificiality, and those girls on the beach, made up in indelible lipsticks and pencils, were all resolved in an infra-human gamut of color, cruel mannequins. As for me, educated by long years of watching a multichromatic Trinitron TV, I observed them without any particular astonishment, taking note of the season's colors, those "natural" tones we believe have been captured *documentarily* when we leaf through a fashion magazine or go to the movies. Perhaps you are unaware that it was French *couturiers* who, in the wake of World War I, imposed the fashion for tanning and spread the fallacy of its healthful effects? Nowadays you'd do well to wonder whether the vivid, blinding yellow of this sun is the same as it always was; perhaps it was launched two seasons ago by an influential fashion house, a "canary yellow" sun, "very youthful"—or whether the greens of the palm trees were "Panzer green" or "Chevalier green." And, of course, for a very long time now we've had a blue that is "Prussian." *Prosit!*

INQUIRY INTO THE NATURE AND CAUSES OF THE WEALTH OF NATIONS. At the end of 1989, I left for the OCCIDENT via Berlin. It was the quickest way to the kingdom of heaven, the only place in the IMPERIUM where the nerves of that other organism were just beneath the skin's surface, just beyond the wall. When the delicate membrane gave way and the two bloods intermingled, Romanian gypsies, Mongols, Bulgarians, Slovaks, and Croats all hurled themselves through the breach: all those who, in the depths of the IMPERIUM, felt the sudden diminution of pressure in their swim bladders and came racing in myriads and droves to prosper in this new ocean.

But in 1989 we were also moving through the prehistory of the amassment of fortunes, the initial accumulation, devoid of Victorian sideburns or the tedious 3 percent per annum. There was oil in Western Siberia, emeralds in the Urals, diamonds in Yakutia, all of them *affaires* of such powerful magnetism that even if you approached them timidly, thousands of kilometers from the golden epicenter, you could become rich between nightfall and dawn.

I needed money; this was the principal correlative to my discovery in the (CHINESE) PALACE, the half-sphere indispensable to achieving the critical mass of full *frivolity*. I went to West Berlin with several kilos of Caspian caviar smuggled in jam pots. (I'm not ashamed to confess this: I had endured long five-year plans in the IMPERIUM, subjected to inhuman budgets of a few rubles per month.) I invested the earnings from that sale in renting a small room and found myself a job washing dishes in a bar: the astonishing automatic dishwasher there, a beautiful and useful machine; the illusion of doing easy work, which in fact was not easy at all. Now I know that I was running the risk of losing my way in a labyrinth of petty expenses where I might have wandered for years, stumbling in the darkness against unpaid invoices and excessively high prices. But one evening, there in the kitchen of that bar, I read a headline in the *Berliner Zeitung* sticking up from the cook's jacket pocket. I plucked it out with my damp fingers. The great news, thanks to which I am here today telling you this story, sipping this 1935

Massandra here in YALTA. (Waiter, please . . . Perfect.)

Verkauf, Inkauf. Easy to decipher. *Verkauf im summer* . . . A plan to auction off quite a bit of pretty decent East German merchandise. To clear kilometers of shelves in preparation for the Bundesrepublik's great leap forward. All the department stores of Dresden, Potsdam and Karl-Marx-Stadt up for sale. For ridiculously low prices! I sat down to ponder the news. The sound of glasses clinking and customers laughing reached me from the bar: workers and small property owners, perhaps a few professionals. Nobodies, in a word, with their small monthly incomes. I went outside, crossed the street, and went into the bar that was opposite. I stayed there for an hour, looking at the buildings, at this other bar. All this could be mine!

And so, well, I managed it. Because I was in on the secret: I knew that to make money, to grow rich, was a virtue. I had passed through the straits of Marxism and rediscovered a simplicity that was Adamic (in the Smithean sense), an excellent theoretical grounding for a more fitting use of the ABACUS. Listen: *All systems, either of preference or restraint, therefore, being thus completely taken away, the obvious and simple system of natural liberty establishes itself of its own accord. Every man, as soon as he does not violate the laws of justice, is left perfectly free to pursue his own interests in his own way, and to bring both his industry and his capital into competition with those of any other man or order of men.* We're saved! I managed to divert the contents of some Leipzig stores into the depths of Eurasia. That was all. Since then, I've chartered airplanes from Southwest Asia, cargo ships full of goods from China.

"Products from Turkey? I've heard there's a real glut of Turkish merchandise."

"No, Chinese merchandise." (The silk route: Bukhara and Samarkand.)

J

JOSIK, JOSHELE, JOSEPH. We sat down next to the windows overlooking the plaza. I said to LINDA, "This is where you exclaim 'I've never seen such a luxurious place before!'"

She glanced up from the menu. "Are you sure you have the money for this?"

"LINDA, I spent more than a year amassing the capital for this novel, thinking about a restaurant like this one (or even finer) and a redheaded girl like you. The budget for the dinner scene is more than adequate, as you'll see. It's only eight p.m. We're just getting started."

LINDA said, "I want to write you a letter."

As if instead of a white tablecloth between us there were kilometers of arid landscape, desert dunes. She insisted. "There are some things I want to tell you."

She wanted to gaze directly into my eyes via the immediacy that only epistolary communication can confer. Allow me to introduce here the first one she wrote that night.

Her first letter, as if from afar.

Hello JOSIK:

This morning I'd been having intense thoughts about a bag of oranges. It's been about half a year since I've eaten an orange. When you told me about your plan, I thought you'd be able to buy lots of them. I don't mean that was the only reason I agreed to go along with you, but sometimes I dream about baskets brimming over with oranges. I would go to Morocco just for the oranges. From any port on the Black Sea we'd be there in five days. We could also eat our fill of bananas. You grew up surrounded by fruit, that's why you're such a good person. I realized this when we were strolling through the garden. I suffer from vitamin deficiencies in the spring; my gums bleed. Even my hair loses its shine. Your teeth are good, too, like a movie star's. We'll make a very good couple in Crimea. I like your plan more and more. Thanks to which I remembered oranges.

Bye.

Nastia

I. The morning after our dinner at the Astoria, Maarif brought me a second letter from LINDA. She never explained why she was writing me again so soon. Apparently Maarif had made a jealous scene, which she brought to a close by punishing him with the task of serving as messenger boy between us. (And thus, after the vulgar fashion of a vulgar love triangle, was the plot thickening.)

Her second letter was full of lies.

Hello JOSHELE:

I have to tell you the truth about my nose. My real last name is Katz. I had a grandfather named Kats or Katz who went to America to make his fortune . . .

It couldn't be true! My pursuit of SOSHA's Hebrew tresses had brought me directly to a Katz! He was from LVOV: Bruno Schulz, Sholem Aleichem, an unexpected twist. I continued reading: *. . . came back ten years later and without so much as going home to give his children a kiss went to the VILLAGE tavern and spent eight hours there, not once stepping outside for a breath of air. He gambled away all his savings at cards, and then, with nothing else* *to wager, his house. That same morning, before day had dawned, someone killed him out of pity. He didn't have enough years of life left to go back to Chicago and save up the money to pay that debt. My grandmother nailed an ace of spades to the coffin and paid two gypsies to lead the funeral procession, throwing out playing cards to the crowd. It was a terrible vengeance. When I think that a quarter of my blood is Hebrew . . .*

Oh, for God's sake, only a quarter . . . But her lovely story was false. She had invented it to mortify Maarif and solidify her relations with me, a foreigner. As if to say: "Look, I've stolen lots of things." She was going to YALTA with me; that was what I gathered from this message. Her decision was irrevocable and she had chosen this extravagant means of conveying it to me.

K

K**. She had the translucent skin of a nocturnal animal. And the way she walked: as if she were trying to steal into the enemy camp, find the silken tent of the sleeping khan, and plunge the silver-handled dagger into his chest. I preferred her to other women because she looked straight into the depths of existence and would formulate questions that were as clear and hard as blocks of ice. Would I be capable of killing someone in order to steal, of killing in cold blood? Clean interrogations, straight from a mind that spun in the void, entirely uncontaminated by any practical matter. She evaluated the possibility of taking drugs or committing suicide in the same way. When we were traveling through Central Asia, I knew she was fully capable of stepping off any train at any unknown stop and disappearing into the STEPPE. I, lying on my cot, the train already back underway, gazing out at the scorched grass in stupefaction.

At first K** didn't want to know I was a writer. The weighty tomes of my VASARI had impressed her, the vast collection of THELONIOUS MONK records, the KLIMT reproductions in my room, but since she thought too much she projected herself far from the insignificance of my articles, the sporadic evidence of certain publications of mine left lying about. When one day the mail brought a magazine containing a story I'd written about our stay at a mountain lake, this was her reaction: "It must be an однофамилец"—*odnofamilets*, someone with the same name—"no?" Which left me speechless. There is no way to object to so simple a refutation. If someone denies your identity, he says to you, "You are not you," and there exists no way of effectively demonstrating the contrary. Show your birth certificate, your identity card? Come on! These are mere pieces of paper. The solemn heart of the matter is that you are not you, you are anyone else but you. I could not convince her that this story was mine, that I was a writer—a beginner, yes, but a writer. Afterward, meditating on it, I reached the conclusion that she was right: the writer was someone else, not me. Wasn't Nabokov, to give an example, someone else? We arrive in a world overflowing with books and are told to believe they've been created by people who are called Nabokov, Conrad, Borges, individuals who evidently had nothing to do with the appearance of books that, nevertheless, we attribute to them. K** would not have believed their assertions, their protests to the contrary, either; if she'd managed to convince me, why wouldn't she have convinced them, too? As a result, I've lived all these years without being a writer. When this ENCYCLOPE-DIA is published I will not be its author, only an *odnofamilets*, someone whose last name I share. Perhaps one day the magic of publicity will succeed in merging us into one and the same man, and then my face alone will suffice to accredit me as a writer, a solution that will be valid only as far as the marketing campaign extends: beyond that I would never be able to prove my condition ontologically. (For K**, the idea of God was not an effect of the existence of God.)

KLINGSOR'S LAST SUMMER (see: ÚLTIMO VERANO DE KLINGSOR).

KLIMT, GUSTAV. In the sense that a mane of hair in the hue known as red ochre held great meaning for me. I'd taken a long while to develop this passion but it had the impact of a sudden awakening when it finally bloomed within me, as when we're no longer hoping for anything from a boring opera and then, in the last act, a backdrop is lowered with a beautiful waterfall or a Chinese pagoda. To discover the splendor of red hair was to set foot for the first time upon the sands of a terra incognita: a new displacement of the soul which, within my sentimental education, acquired the worth of a pilgrimage to Tibet.

I. At a spot along Nevsky Prospekt, LINDA, who, as I would later learn, was named Anastasia Stárseva, was waiting for me. She'd been playing the FLUTE in the portal of the Kazan Cathedral and THELONIOUS stopped to listen to her. Moved, he thought of the MAGIC FLUTE and his adolescent years, and allowed himself to be carried off by the FLUTE's trill, the human warmth of its metallic resonance. When he reopened his eyes onto that morning—Saint Petersburg, the cathedral's colonnade—he discovered in surprise that a halo surrounded the flautist. Then he took a closer look and was left mute with astonishment. This was LINDA's skin. As if it had been deliberately stretched across her cheeks in such a way as to retract, while she blew into the FLUTE, without forming any wrinkles, assimilating itself into the depths. Only a slight intensification of tone to a deeper red gave away the work of that skin, the subcutaneous flow of blood. (In winter, cheeks like that, brushstrokes of bright red applied by the HARD FROST, embellished the vestibule of a movie theater where we'd taken refuge to warm up: the vivid bloom of a naive doll's painted face. Then a gradual return to a pale pink that bespoke such freshness, a quality that belonged to the centuries before the habit of sunbathing became widespread, and that was very well suited to the still life V** and I comprised, stretched out on the bed: the sheet's heavy folds, the leaden gray of a vase, the inchoate drift of our disarticulated limbs, dark against pale.)

After a short pause, the flautist attacked a march with great resolve—the happy tremolo—then almost immediately interrupted her playing to remove her warm woolen cap. A luxuriant mass of red hair, rolled into locks thick as snakes, fell in cascades over her back, shoulders, chest. (*Oh how well doth a fair colour and a brilliant sheen upon the glittering hair! Behold it encountereth with the beams of the sun like swift lightning, or doth softly reflect them back again, or changeth clean contrary into another grace. Sometimes the beauty of the hair, shining like gold, resembles the colour of honey; sometimes, when it is raven black, the blue plume and azure feathers about the necks of does, especially when it is anointed with the nard of Arabia, or trimly tuffed out with the teeth of a fine comb; and if it be tied up in the nape of the neck, it seemeth to the lover that beholdeth the same as a glass that yieldeth forth a more pleasant and gracious comeliness.* —*The Golden Ass,* Being the Metamorphoses of Lucius Apuleius, translated by William Adlington.) MONK stops short, fears he will lose his footing and topple into the abyss at his feet, and quickly raises his eyes beyond this splash of red ochre, locating the bridge with its winged lions, the canal's gray parapet, to rest them there a while, the girl forgotten in the depths of his peripheral vision. His calm regained, he courageously resolves to focus his gaze on her once more: the apparition of Venus on the seashell, a chorus of little angels, their cheeks puffed out, blowing. A vision that filled MONK with indescribable tenderness: the great God who has placed another portion of that BREAD . . .

I wonder if THELONIOUS would ever have discovered LINDA if not for the miracle of that music. Be that as it may, he decides to follow her. He watches her pick up the hat full of small change, then separate the FLUTE into three parts and return them to their case; he watches her take the arm of her friend in the overcoat and walk away from the cathedral toward Nevsky Prospekt . . .

KVAS. Russia is an old country with strange fermented beverages and barrel staves lying in the mud. I jump from stave to stave to keep my boots from getting dirty, while dogs bark behind fences. At the corner—this city on the Volga where I've come to spend a few weeks, these low brick buildings—the same woman as yesterday is pouring out KVAS.

L

LENIN (*the swine*). "A man's at the door for you, quite the BRODIAGA," RUDI murmurs in my ear.

I went out to the lobby. The rain had stopped and the day was still as bright as it had been at six that evening. I recognized my baggage handler's checked jacket and black cap.

"Dimitri!"

"(It's Kolia.)"

"Kolia!" I turned to the doorman. "He's a friend."

"However did you find me? What a surprise! Come in and join us; no one will mind."

Touched that I hadn't put him out in the street, he lied, "I've been thinking about you all day."

"Say no more," I patted his back in an expansive gesture as if I were the owner of many a десятина of land and muzhiks in abundance.

The duchess studied him from behind the nonexistent monocle of her asperity. To the already questionable fact of having agreed to share a table with strangers was now added the inclusion of this personage, who bore a distinct resemblance to the sort of family man who ducks out of the house to fritter away his salary drinking wine next to fences.

Maarif, however, gave no sign of discontent. He had remained silent since his arrival. Now he was watching the general, who ate with ancestral appetite, as if he were just back from a difficult maneuver in the Sea of Barents. Maarif observed him ingesting the lustrous morsel of an anchovy, a small and agile dolphin lost between the general's

71

crunching mandibles, his wire-rimmed glasses in the foreground shooting off alarming sparks and belying the faint smile on his lips. His
thick fingers. Another little fish. A long swig of Aqua vitae, *vodochka*.
(And the army of workers and peasants clambering over the bars of
the Winter Palace, overthrowing the two-headed eagle.) Which was
more or less what Maarif said, something like: October was not in
vain, the fight to eradicate the weed of insatiable gluttony. The leader
of that revolution, comrade . . .

At the sudden explosion of the word Lenin, Kolia's eyes went blank
as if a great rage had possessed him. He leapt to his feet and began
striking his glass with a fork: "*Gentlemen!* Но, Господа (*Gospoda*)! And
forgive me if I offend anyone by calling you that. Be aware that I cannot
speak the word with any degree of assurance, and without a feeling of
falsity, but I refuse to insult you with the word товáрищ"—*tovarish*
or comrade—"though perhaps the general . . ."

"No, that's fine. *Gospada!* As in the old days: *Gospada ofitseri!*"
(Meaning "*Señores oficiales!*" or "Esteemed officers!")

a) The imperium in full-blown identity crisis. The TV had opened
up the debate on how to address strangers in the street. There were
certain hesitations regarding *gospodin*—its literal meaning, "master,"
sounded offensive to some ears—and, too, over *citizen*, which conferred
the stigma of not being a *tovarish:* "Release that billy club, citizen, you
are under arrest." Some had opted for сударь (*sudar*)—"sir"—which
was far too nineteenth-century, while the simplest people, vendors
in the bazaars, had decided to stick with a term that left no room for
doubt: мужчúна (*muzhina*), meaning, simply and plainly, *man.* Since
all these forms of address entrained the insecurity of wearing someone else's finery, I had seen polite, well-bred people recite each one
in sequence, beginning with the stigmatized *tovarish* and ending with
the laughable *gentleman.* (For years the phrase "Russian *gentleman*"

had been winning all competitions for who could come up with the shortest joke. "Once there was a Russian *gentleman* . . ." And that was it. That was the joke.)

"*Gospada!* LENIN . . . No, it's incredible. If I told you that LENIN . . . Well . . . The great deception, *gospada!* Have you all heard about the letter that was kept secret from us? Listen: there exists a letter from Marx in which he explained that the Communist experiment could not be carried out in our little Mother Russia. A letter perfidiously concealed from us by the Russian Marxists, by the *bolcheviki,* may the devil take them! And think about this, *gospada!* Everything around us was LENIN. A veritable scourge. The Metro, the main avenues, the streets of the most insignificant VILLAGES, the young LENINIST pioneers who went on to swell the ranks of the LENINIST Komsomol. I'm astonished not to find here, at the entrance to this lovely restaurant, a plaque stating that LENIN had lunch here on the afternoon of December 6, 1903, upon his return from exile in Siberia. And the falsehoods we were told about the penuries he supposedly experienced there! Ah, but they never explained how people lived in the VILLAGES during the time of the CZARS. Allow me to inform you: a veritable land of Cockaigne. A golden age when the peasants greased the axles of their wagons with butter . . . Ah, well . . . I was acquainted with the terrible Siberia of the Gulag. I was born in a forced labor camp and grew up among prisoners of conscience, for I was a real victim of the system, *gospoda!* I don't want to spoil your dinner, but think about that. This young man . . . When I heard this young fellow say his name . . . I . . ."

b) Kolia turned out to be one of those philosophical BRODIAGAS who wander about the IMPERIUM. For a short period he had lived at the Nikolaevsky Station (Vronsky and Karenina: the morning mist) where he spent months reading these terrible truths while sipping TEA from the samovar of an out-of-service passenger car. He had descended into the entrails of the deception, penetrating its deepest geological strata, and discovered a vast deposit of busts of LENIN, the caryatids upon which the vault of the IMPERIUM rested. Every day new truths were published about the brief meter and sixty centimeters that LENIN's body had measured: we had learned of the lover who died of typhus in 1920 (that part we'd suspected: Nadezhda Krupskaya was just too horrible), his dreadful taste in literature . . .

"And believe me, *gospada,* the years I spent in Afghanistan, where I risked my precious life—*ta-ta-ta-ta-ta*! Run, Kolia!—chased by desert bedouins . . . I'd crossed the border in secret and was carrying a very important dispatch to our man in Kabul. And was constantly chased by those bedouins on their ships of the desert that look slow but in fact are very fast, those camels . . . Ah, why fatigue you? Your poor and humble servant successfully got past three enemy blockades, arrived at our embassy in Kabul on the verge of collapse, and managed to say 'I have an important dispatch from Moscow' before falling limp against the grille. Then the sentry looked out at me from between the heavy bars and shouted, 'Show your identification,' and what he meant was my party card: 'Demonstrate, in some way, your loyalty to the regime.' Imagine my amazement, *gospada!* I who was fighting in defense of little Mother Russia, and here these followers of LENIN, the swine . . . In a word, I was taken prisoner by the bedouins and spent five years in captivity. I learned to speak their language. Of course . . ."—and he stared fixedly at RUDI, our waiter. "Salaam!" he proffered and made a deep genuflection, for he hated RUDI and therefore didn't mind humiliating himself with that false demonstration.

"You're mistaken, Kolia," I told him. "RUDI is Moldavian, a land of magnificent wines. I don't see why . . ."

But Kolia had recovered his composure. "Yes, well, you're right. It's just that those scallywags from the Caucasus have invaded our cities . . . But that's not worth talking about. Instead, let's toast our glorious army."

"A toast!" I shouted, too, like a Muscovite.

LIFT. The people of Russia suffer from a compulsion to inventory the cosmos and make everything within it intelligible. The Bolsheviks, fervent adepts of social engineering, loved definitions so exhaustive that they left all meaning entirely dessicated. Every Metro car bore a plaque in minuscule text: "How to make use of the Metropolitan underground rail system." The elevators (called *LIFTS* in Russian, too), those "infernal machines," are also equipped with extensive instructions. Those for the elevator in my building read like this (as I waited for the LIFT I would read the text again and again, hypnotized):

REGULATIONS FOR USAGE OF THE
PASSENGER ELEVATOR
(Weight Limit: 500 kg or six persons)

1. *This elevator is intended for the transportation of passengers, furniture, and other objects of quotidian use.*
2. *To summon the empty car, activate the button located next to its entrance on every floor, on the external side. After the call button has been pressed, wait for the car to arrive.*
3. *When the car arrives at the floor from which the call was made, the doors of both the elevator shaft and the car will open automatically.*
4. *Enter the elevator or place your cargo inside it without delay. If the doors close too soon, it will be necessary to press the call button again.*
5. *After entering or completing the loading of cargo into the car,*

*press the button (situated on the panel in the interior of the car)
for the desired floor. The doors will close automatically and the
car will begin to move. In case of surcharge, the* SURCHARGE
*light will illuminate on the control panel and the car will not
begin to move.*

6. *Upon arrival at the desired floor, the doors will open automatically.*

7. *Should the elevator function defectively, press the* STOP *button
for an emergency stop.*

IT IS FORBIDDEN

8. *To attempt to accelerate or in any way tamper with the movement
of the automatic doors, and to lean against them.*

9. *To attempt to open the doors when the car is in motion.*

10. *To attempt to open the doors of a malfunctioning elevator on
one's own. Such a procedure is extremely dangerous.*

11. *To open the trap door in the roof of the elevator.*

12. *For preschool children to travel on the elevator without being
accompanied by an adult.*

13. *To load the elevator with flammable liquids or objects of large
dimension.*

14. *To smoke in the elevator.*

*Let us take good care of the elevator. Do not permit mischief by children,
vandalism by adolescents, or mistreatment of the elevator by adults!*

(I always thought that one piece of chilling advice was missing:
*When the doors of the elevator open, please ascertain that the floor is there
prior to entering.*)

More about elevators: "The Angel of the Bridge," by John Cheever.

LIGHT OF OTHER DAYS, THE. In close-up a movie screen is not the homogenous canvas we imagine from our seats in the ninth row but a sheet of polyvinyl riddled with minuscule orifices almost invisible to the eye. Thus we see only a small percentage of the projected image; a great part of it passes through these tiny orifices and lands in the terrifying void behind the screen. When the brick wall that stands back there reaches a certain level of saturation, a process of spontaneous emission of all the films projected over the years takes place. Since the force of this emission rarely exceeds in energy that of the primary emission—the one from the projector—the phenomenon was only quite recently discovered. In the mid-seventies, Kliuchariov and Alimushkin, two BRODIAGAS who've now become famous, chose to spend a cold winter night in an abandoned movie theater on Nevsky Prospekt. At three in the morning, unable to sleep because of the excess of light that flowed across the screen, they discovered a phosphorescent flickering of inverted forms on the polyvinyl. The inexplicable nature of the phenomenon meant that the secret had to be kept for almost two decades. This fortunate interdiction spared us extensive monographs on the lousy movies of the 1930s and the ag-itprop films of the 1920s. Now, in 1991, titles from 1918 "and on" (that is to say, and earlier) have begun to appear. The face of one beautiful woman in particular persists against the white background.

I. In 1910, four years before the premiere of *Song of Triumphant Love,* her apotheosis, Vera Vasilievna, the future great star of Russian silent film (one of those butterflies of pleated ORGANDY at her waist), took special care to exchange the crude fetter of her hard maiden name of Levchenko for the alluring and exotic double-stranded necklace of Холодная (Kholodnaya). When this name, full of soft *a*s and *o*s, was murmured in every salon in Muscovy, many imagined it to be a very apt pseudonym. In Russian, *kholodnaya* means "cold woman," and Vera Lánina, the adulterous beauty she played in *At the Fireside,* was indeed cold and distant. Russia's so-called "Silver Age" (another lovely name) had had its tastes distorted by Игорь Северянин (Igor *Severyanin*, a pen name meaning "Northerner"), Андрей Бе́лый (Andrei *Biely*, whose chosen pseudonym was "White"), and Са́ша Чёрный (Sasha *Chorny*, or "Black," another nom de plume). Thus when, after *At the Fireside*, everyone flocked to her next film, *Forget Your Home, the Fire There No Longer Burns*, no one was inclined to lend the slightest credence to the hypothesis that Kholodnaya was simply her married name.

a) This quaintly antiquated vogue for pseudonyms has a fossil: Иосиф Виссарионович Сталин (Joseph Vissarionovich Stalin, whose adopted monicker means "man of steel").

For her husband, Vladimir Kholodny, the name had no exotic meaning: what's more, he was the editor of Авто or *Auto* (*Steam and Speed*) the first Russian magazine for car enthusiasts. Vera Vasilievna Levchenko, too, seems to have had a taste for technological novelty. Four years later, metamorphosed into "the queen of the screen," she drove only the latest model Renaults for her appearances in *Daughter of the Century, Why Do I Love So Madly?* and *The Chess Game of Life*.

b) Already in 1918 automobiles summoned notions of power and strength. Trotsky scandalized Moses Nappelbaum, a portraitist whose studio was on Nevsky Prospekt, by having his picture taken in a chauffeur's uniform adorned with leather and buckles, precisely the attire that would become characteristic of the civil war's terrible commisars.

In 1914, with the outbreak of world war, the fiery glances and heavily retouched eyes of Lyda Borelli and Francesca Bertini suddenly caught on in Moscow. That same year, Vera Kholodnaya, a complete unknown, appeared in the offices of *gospodín* Khanzhonkov, a magnate of the nascent film industry. Vera Vasilievna signed a five-year contract with Khanzhonkov, without suspecting that this *gospodin* was the devil and she would die at the end of that period.

She acted in forty-seven films of love and despair. Her heroines' laughter always contained a note of sadness: Pola, the unhappy acrobat, who executed dangerous moves and one night lost her grip on the trapeze, flew across the tent, and fell, luxuriously dressed—in a hat adorned with ostrich feathers—into a beautiful Muscovite mansion.

On October 25, by the old calendar, *The Human Beast* premiered (that cinema on Nevsky Prospekt still exhibits the film's poster, behind glass). This prophetic title was followed in that season's program, as we can see, by others no less foreboding: *Wounded Soul, Be Silent My Sadness*, and finally a filmed version of a story by Tolstoy that was a true premonition: *The Living Corpse.*

When the contract ended in 1919 it was easier to die of typhoid fever than of *La Española*, the flu pandemic with a name that sounded like one of her melodramas, the last one, and that killed La Kholodnaya on February 16 at the age of twenty-five.

LINDA EVANGELISTA. As if I were called THELONIOUS MONK and she were LINDA EVANGELISTA.

I knew how to lead a false existence under those names; we had only to believe in our metamorphosis, leap onto the magic carpet of a perfect life, and contemplate from there the ciphers that denoted a bad year, any bad year—1990, 1991—as if it were 1819 or 1099 or some other historically significant combination of numerals, viewed from a distance.

I'd discovered the name in *Vogue* one afternoon as I was analyzing the season's latest accessories with all the interest and archaeological passion of a scholar who specializes in Greek togas. The alias was so perfectly suited to my project that I never hesitated for a second to make use of it. Moreover, there was LINDA herself, whom I encountered swimming in the fragrance of a page impregnated with OPIUM. I still have the pictures: LINDA poses beneath the arch of a dark medieval bridge, as if abandoned there by a perverse djinni out of the *Thousand and One Nights*. She is gazing into the distance toward a love, an impossible love, and, in a gesture of farewell, has extended arms that are covered in dazzling fake gems. Heavy chains emphasize her waist; their sparkle heightens the black of a dress that clings to her body like "a second skin" but which, from the hips down, floats into airy flights of tulle, a sfumato through whose transparences can be seen, in fierce outline, LINDA EVANGELISTA's swooningly perfect legs: fishnet stockings, a capricious pair of pointy-toed pumps. An invitation to buy a few of Yves Saint Laurent's atomizers and also perchance to reflect upon the fleeting nature of our earthly existence.

For I would never be able to encompass all the women who floated toward me down Nevsky Prospekt, each a captive within the watertight bubble of her own beauty.

Тысячи сортов шляпок, платьев, платков,—пестрых, легких, к которым иногда в течение целых двух дней сохраняется привязанность их владетельниц, ослепят хоть кого на Невском проспекте. Кажется, как будто целое море мотыльков поднялось вдруг со стеблей и волнуется блестящею тучею над черными жуками мужеского пола . . . А какие встретите вы дамские рукава на Невском проспекте! Ах, какая прелесть! Они несколько похожи на два воздухоплавательные шара, так что дама вдруг бы поднялась на воздух, если бы не поддерживал ее мужчина; потому что даму так же легко и приятно поднять на воздух, как подносимый ко рту бокал, наполненный шампанским.

(Which is to say: *Thousands of varieties of hats, dresses, and kerchiefs, flimsy and bright-colored, for which their owners feel sometimes an adoration that lasts two whole days, dazzle everyone on Nevsky Prospekt. A whole sea of butterflies seems to have flown up from their flower stalks and to be floating in a glittering cloud above the beetles of the male sex . . . And the ladies' sleeves that you meet on Nevsky Prospekt! Ah, how exquisite! They are like two balloons and the lady might suddenly float up into the air, were she not held down by the gentleman accompanying her; for it would be as easy and agreeable for a lady to be lifted into the air as for a glass of champagne to be lifted to the lips.* ——"Nevsky Prospekt," Nikolai Vasilievich Gogol, translated by Constance Garnett.)

I was consoled by the sheer quantity of beauties I saw, each one so perfect, and they came to merge into a single being; their multiplicity —like the innumerable apparitions of LINDA, the real LINDA, in that same issue of *Vogue*: strolling through a meadow in a yellow jacket and matching skirt, wearing a leopard-print cap and shirt; coming through the door of an artist's studio dressed in strict tweeds; drinking cocktails next to a swimming pool's fathomless blue, her striped bathrobe falling open—was merely apparent; in essence they were all the same woman. I imagined LINDA, my heroine, as the mathematical average of all the beautiful women I'd known in Russia, their profiles superimposed. I believed that there, along Nevsky Prospekt, I would find the woman I was seeking, and as you shall see I was not mistaken. So many Russian women are so beautiful!

Next to the Imperial Theater, I discovered a fresh face in the crowd. A specimen with sweet eyes beneath delicate brows. It might be LINDA. She moved forward without relaxing her straight shoulders, her gaze cast down, pressing a slim portfolio against her chest. I radioed my urgent message to her but she passed without detecting the signals that I, a lighthouse in deep fog, was sending out. I turned to watch her walk away. She was almost what I was looking for. Her hair.

The girl with the slim portfolio was immediately replaced by others, all equally beautiful: blondes with soft faces, sharp-profiled women with light brown hair. Standing there as they streamed by, I let myself bathe in those faces and envelop each one in a story that took shape from the point zero of a pair of lips, a gesture, the Asiatic cast of a cheekbone, a story that would flash across my mind—maritime excursions, dancing until dawn—to burn out in an instant, its mistress borne off on the waters of that human river.

LONDON DANDY, THE. To Nabokov, Onegin, Pushkin's alter ego, is not a dandy in the pure sense of the term. In his annotated translation of *Eugene Onegin* (New York, 1956) Nabokov cites the following line from *The Life of George Brummell Esq., Commonly Called Beau Brummell:* "Brummell most assuredly was no dandy. He was a beau . . . His chief aim was to avoid anything marked," adding, "Onegin, too, was a beau and not a dandy." A distinction that strikes me as misguided and that seems to have been dictated by the slightly pejorative sense of the word "dandy" to the Russian ear. I don't believe Pushkin himself would have accepted Nabokov's dictum. His dandy-ism was as elemental as his way of breathing in French, though he did not imitate Brummell's practice of sandpapering the silk of his brand-new suits to eliminate the shine in order to wear them with nonchalance. Pushkin's biographers also fail to mention any invention on his part of a new type of buckle for his shoes. Nevertheless, the poet managed to coin a phrase—Денди лондонский, *Dendi londonski*—that would take on singular importance for his cold country, the extension of Asia. And that fact is of greater weight and consequence than Beau Brummell's innocent shoe buckle. It was a title of nobility, the iron cross sported by those who boasted of belonging to the species *homo occidentalis,* the Russian *ʒapadniki* (or Westerners). (Technically PETER I was the first *ʒapadnik* and *arbitrum elegantiarum* of Eurasia. Not content with shaving the boyars' beards and dressing them in European fashion, he was led by a pure and metaphysical dandy-ism to build a city for himself in much the same way one orders a bespoke suit.) This *homo occidentalis* disappeared into the depths of the Gulag toward the end of the 1920s and reappeared, intact, during the *thaw;* this time beneath the inoffensive aspect of Moscow's *stiliagi,* a tribe of Apaches who greased their hair and wore pointed shoes, all of them deserters from the clearing of the Virgin Lands.

I do not know whether Nabokov—another authentic specimen of *homo occidentalis* who was traveling across the American Midwest in a beautiful PACKARD driven by his wife during that period—greased his hair or wore tortoiseshell glasses. But I take it for granted that he was very well acquainted with the memoirs of Avdotya Panaeva. I read them because they offer curious glimpses of the figures who visited her salon (a young F.M., madly in love with the hostess, Turgenev and Chadeyev, each the epitome of the dandy). Panaeva writes that, as a girl, she once saw Pushkin at the opera. Nothing in her description of him supports Nabokov's assertion that Pushkin would have avoided "anything marked."

. . . однажды, в театре, сидела я в ложе с сестрами и братьями и с одной из теток. Почти к последнему акту в соседнюю ложу, где сидели две дамы и старичок, вошел курчавый, бледный и худощавый мужчина. Я сейчас же заметила, что у него на одном пальце надето что-то вроде золотого наперстка. Это меня заинтересовало. Мне казалось, что его лицо мне знакомо. Курчавый господин зевал, потягивался и не смотрел на сцену, а глядел больше на ложи, отвечал нехотя, когда с ним заговаривали дамы по-французски. Вдруг я припомнила, где я его видела, и, дернув тетку за рукав, шепнула ей: "сзади нас сидит Пушкин". Я потому его не сразу узнала, что никогда не видела его без шляпы. Но Пушкин скоро ушел изложи. Более мне не удалось его видеть. Уже взрослой я узнала значение золотого наперстка на его пальце. Он отрастил себе большой ноготь и, чтоб последний не сломался, надевал золотой футляр.

Once I was sharing a box at the opera with my sisters and one of my aunts. Before the last act, a slender gentleman, very pale and with curly hair, made an entrance into the neighboring box. Immediately I noticed a kind of golden thimble on one of his fingers that greatly intrigued me. Moreover, his face seemed familiar. The gentleman with curly hair yawned and stretched, gazing at the other boxes, paying no attention to what was happening onstage, and answering listlessly when the ladies spoke to him in French. Suddenly, I remembered where I had seen him. I tugged at my aunt's arm and whispered: "We have Pushkin behind us." I hadn't recognized him because it was the first time I'd seen him without a hat. After a while Pushkin left the box and I never saw him again. As an adult, I learned what he used that thimble for. He had let the nail of his pinky finger grow long and used the golden thimble to protect it.

M

MAGNUS, ALBERTUS. At seven p.m. I proceeded downstairs to the Astoria's restaurant to finalize the details of our dinner. I found the waiter who would be serving us that night in the kitchen, shining his shoes. He answered to the alias of RUDI and I spoke with him a while to make sure he would know how to play his role. He listened to me with his face turned toward the floor, spying on me through his thick eyebrows: RUDI, a HAM of the Transcaucasus. In the dining room, I showed him a table for six next to a large window and told him I expected a fresh tablecloth. I removed a heavy candlestick from the center of the table and in its place arranged pieces of glass fruit next to every setting. For the time being, only LINDA and I were on the guest list, but it's an easy matter to assemble six people around a table in the Grand Duchy of Muscovy: Russian spontaneity.

I. Back in the lobby—hands in my pockets—I was struck by one of those flat, two-dimensional mannequins made from a photo blown up to life size that a travel agency was exhibiting in the corridor. It seemed to be part of a campaign to promote tourism in Southeast Asia. The model's makeup was powerfully exotic: a white mask, pale as plaster, lips of the most vivid violet, a penciled-on beauty spot. From afar, the woman seemed to be offering something (a pair of tickets?) in her extended right hand. As I approached the mannequin I bent forward to *study it,* my eyes fixed on its eyes, which were staggeringly realistic. In the dim light of that hour, they had the translucent green of those unfathomable human gazes in which we lose our way, wavering between the eyes and the point of light reflected within them, or else they were as vacant as the holes that serve as the eyes of a fairground colossus, filled in by the faces of tourists who are the iris and the pupils. I discovered that what she had in her hand was one of the heavy knobs to which the hotel's room keys were attached, and immediately the smiling girl became a Japanese reminder placed there by the hotel management to admonish forgetful guests who would sometimes leave the hotel still carrying their keys. Calmer now, I lowered my eyes and brought them to rest on her chest and its admirably lifelike flesh color (but why admirable? a mere photographic illusion). Still half-leaning toward her, I suddenly perceived a growing flutter, a slight agitation, a crinkle of printed silk, and my ear captured the faint whistle of air expanding through her breast. Then, into the heart of the mystery, breaking the shell of air that surrounded me, a *vox* descended and called my name: "JOSUÉ! JOSUÉ! Wake up for God's sake!" In a flash I thought, "Yes, wake up to reality, to real life! Now, and for all time!" Shaken by this truth, I rose through the clots of air, raised my eyes and . . . it was LINDA! For the love of God! LINDA! I stared at her another fraction of a second without understanding a thing, still shaken (to the very core of my being), reorganizing my hemispheres, returning the scattered blocks of consciousness to their place. Back in the lobby of the Astoria, in Saint Petersburg, in 1991, I understood that LINDA was seeking to put my nerves to the test with her disconcerting rediscovery of the polychromatic nature of ancient Greek statuary. But how many years would it be before the rest of us caught up to the daring color combination that LINDA was trying out that evening?

Many, many years. Her taste was astonishingly developed, as I already knew (it wasn't a question of having or not having good taste). She'd imagined I would scold her in annoyance: "My God, you've been playing the flute since you were seven but you still don't know how to put makeup on?" It surprised her when I explained patiently how futile her little last-minute protest was.

"LINDA, the dress is yours, it's a gift."

"You're completely inconsistent! Your thesis . . . The novel you say you're writing . . ."

"It's because I had warmer tones in mind for you. Look at this print. Why do you need more color? I'll wait for you to change your makeup, but you must do it quickly. It's almost eight."

"знаеш!" In her indignation she switched automatically into a harder form of Russian. "*Znaesh!*" (She meant: "Know what? I can walk out of here right now.") She drew a breath. "Give me back the pictures!"

Ay, I was expecting this! I took out the Polaroids and held them in front of her eyes like a man about to plunge a piece of litmus paper into the test solution. LINDA changed color beneath her mask and stared at them in fascination. "It's as if years had gone by, as if they were very old pictures," she murmured.

That was what she said, in a very small thread of voice. "It's as if years had gone by . . ." I wasn't expecting such a crushing reaction. A devastating chill advanced along my spine and LINDA's smooth face became impenetrable once more. She raised her eyes slowly to ask me another question, to tell me something I could no longer hear and her two obols flecked with green and black settled a cold gaze upon me, a gaze that was *inhuman*, unblinking.

II. In biographies of Thomas Aquinas we find the same alarm followed with sudden rage triggered by a serious mistake on the part of his mentor, Albertus Magnus: the automaton or alchemical doll. Allow me to explain: the construction of an android is a false path, a dead end by which we will never reach the SUMMA TECHNOLOGIAE. It offers a mechanical solution—creation not in the image but in the semblance—when the true solution verges on ghostliness, the generation of a mental world created entirely out of such stuff as dreams are made on.

(Necesse est ponere aliquas creaturas incorporeas. Id enim quod prae-cipue in rebus creatis Deus intendit est bonum quod consistit in as-similatione ad Deum. Perfecta autem assimilatio effectus ad causam attenditur, quando effectus imitatur causam secundum illud per quod causa producit effectum; sicut calidum facit calidum. Deus autem creaturam producit per intellectum et voluntatem, ut supra ostensum est. Unde ad perfectionem universi requiritur quod sint aliquae crea-turae intellectuales. Intelligere autem non potest esse actus corporis, nec alicuius virtutis corporeae, quia omne corpus determinatur ad hic et nunc. Unde necesse est ponere, ad hoc quod universum sit perfectum, quod sit aliqua incorporea creatura.)

(Or: *There must be some incorporeal creatures. For what is principally intended by God in creatures is good, and this consists in assimilation to God Himself. And the perfect assimilation of an effect to a cause is accomplished when the effect imitates the cause according to that whereby the cause produces the effect; as heat makes heat. Now, God produces the creature by His intellect and will. Hence the perfection of the universe requires that there should be intellectual creatures. Now intelligence cannot be the action of a body, nor of any corporeal faculty, for every body is limited to "here" and "now." Hence the perfection of the universe requires the existence of an incorporeal creature. —Treatise on the Angels* (QQ [50] a. 1, Saint Thomas Aquinas, translated by Fathers of the English Dominican Province)

MASTER AND MARGARITA, THE (Мáстер и Маргарѝта). "Listen, we have makeup experts who can spend a whole hour just preparing the face for a normal workday. You'll have to get through a short trial period during which we decide whether or not to hire you, but that will be better for you than playing the FLUTE at the cathedral. We'll be working on the outskirts of Saint Petersburg —there are extremely beautiful spots there; ever visited the (CHINESE) PALACE?—and then, if you really are what we're looking for (and I'm almost sure you are), we'll travel south, to YALTA, for a cover photo—redheads are big this year. The work will be exhausting, I'm warning you, but there are a lot of girls who'd give almost anything to be in your place.

"You never wanted to be a model? You think it's a job for women who are stupid? You're wrong. There is an intelligence in beauty, a true feeling that can alter the silhouette of a pair of legs, penetrate the occult meaning of rouge and expensive face creams. What interests me is the possibility of removing you from your animal state, endowing you with eyes that will allow you to contemplate the world in a more precise way. This will be easy; you have the natural intelligence of your red hair. A while ago, as I watched you playing in the cathedral, nothing in your face, neither your speckled eyes nor your Slavic cheekbones, caught my attention. Everything changed, as you know, when I watched your hair fall over your shoulders.

"I seek to expand the borders of the moment, to capture all signals, painstakingly, to stop the passage of time in a perfect second of heightened perception: the pleasing touch of a linen shirt, your full, arched eyebrows, the breeze that dries us off after a warm bath. It's as if I were to tempt you with immortality, though I am not an emissary from the devil. Notice my shoes. Aren't they beautiful? The signals arrive in such profusion and are so dissimilar that they demand a keen eye, a highly trained intelligence."

(I patted my portfolio.) "I have here a dossier I've been assembling for several months. I'll keep the photos I've taken of you today here, too, so that half a year from now you can see yourself as you once were. You'll be amazed at how vague your eyes were, without the fixity of a subtler appreciation, a purer decanting. I'm sure you'll get there soon. That's what I'm here for. The main thing is to meet the person who can give you this kind of polish. It will be as if I were teaching you to sing and, in fact, that's exactly what I want to do: nuance the voice of your gaze, your bearing, so you won't be swept along by your natural tone, but will build constructions that shift at every moment, leave an empty space, create a hollow that then becomes your voice, which hits a note that rings from a thousand points like one of those amazing singers of *spirituals*.

"In fact, I must now confess: I don't actually work for a fashion house. But that in no way alters the meaning of my invitation. I deal in real life; I seek to confer upon it the luster of a finished product, ready for the marketplace. I move the clouds in the sky, add light and air to distant vistas, accentuate the green of trees and lawns, seek to awaken a reality that will be more blue and more red. This is a private initiative, and I require a woman, a redhead such as yourself, to help me bring the project to a successful conclusion. You had already almost agreed to pose for a fashion magazine. What I'm proposing is that you *pose* for this novel. It amounts to the same thing, essentially. In fact it's better, because you'll actually experience everything that's generally left outside the frame in photography. Okay, I know that in the OCCIDENT very rich models make two million dollars a year and wouldn't see the life you'll lead as even remotely luxurious. That's just a detail, a small incongruence of scale. You'll get used to it, LINDA," I said, calling her by her name for the first time. "It's as if you'd been working at a soda fountain or a cheap café and were discovered there and cast in the role of *The Rise and Rise of the Girl from Nowhere*."

She had been listening attentively but then let out a shriek. "My God, something's happening to your shoes!"

As if abandoned there on the gravel and entirely alien to me, my BOOGIE SHOES were emitting a fluorescent glow that pulsated more intensely from time to time. In just a few seconds they grew to several times their normal size and stretched all the way across the path, inflating to a malevolent roundness.

I. That same voice, previously: ". . . though I'm not an emissary from the devil." (An entirely superfluous justification.) The MASTER who, weakened by a strange malady, knows his death is approaching and makes a pact with the devil. For a while now, THELONIOUS has toyed with the idea of an essay on *frivolity*, and has disposed of the amount of whalebone necessary to elaborate a *Tractatus* (Basel, 1650). Finally, he decided upon an essay in the primitive sense of the word: an alchemical experiment. To mix all his dandified knowledge within the vessel of a young soul, to bequeath his vision to an innocent girl. To gain her consent, THELONIOUS tempts her with a model's life and even resorts to a brief demonstration of his alchemical powers, transforming his shoes before her eyes. Булга́ков (Bulgakov), in THE MASTER AND MARGARITA, describes a similar scene, from which I excerpt this passage:

Удивленная Маргарита Николаевна повернулась и увидела на своей скамейке гражданина, который, очевидно, бесшумно подсел в то время, когда Маргарита загляделась на процессию и, надо полагать, в рассеянности вслух задала свой последний вопрос . . .

Рыжий оглянулся и сказал таинственно:

—Меня прислали, чтобы вас сегодня вечером пригласить в гости.

—Что вы бредите, какие гости? . . .

—К одному очень знатному иностранцу—значительно
сказал рыжий, прищурив глаз . . .

—Я приглашаю вас к иностранцу совершенно безопасному.
И ни одна душа не будет знать об этом посещении. Вот уж
за это я вам ручаюсь.

—А зачем я ему понадобилась?—вкрадчиво спросила
Маргарита.

—Вы об этом узнаете позже.

—Понимаю . . . Я должна ему отдаться—сказала
Маргарита задумчиво.

MARGARITA Nikolayevna turned with a start and found an indi-
vidual beside her on the bench. He must have taken advantage of her
absorption in the procession —the same absorption that had made
her speak her question aloud—to sit down there.

The red-haired man looked around, then said in a mysterious tone,
"I've been sent here to deliver an invitation for this evening to you."

"You must be mad. What sort of invitation?"

"An invitation to the home of a very illustrious foreigner," said
the red-haired stranger, narrowing one eye with an air of great sig-
nificance. "I'm inviting you to the home of a foreign gentleman who
can do you no harm. Furthermore, no one will be aware of your visit.
You have my word on that.

"And what does he need me for?" MARGARITA asked timidly.

"You'll learn that in time."

"I understand . . . I must let him have his way with me," said
MARGARITA pensively.

In the end, Azazello, emissary of Woland, the devil, gives MAR-
GARITA a magical unguent that will enable her to fly. THELONIOUS, too,
will one day fly, before LINDA's astonished eyes.

MEMORY BUFFER. It's an instant of seeing yourself from the outside,
holding your breath while it happens. It allows us to postpone, for a
thousandth of a second, the experience of the smiling face, and receive
it steadily, free of the trembling of our hands. It allows for a minimum
interval of certainty between the eye and the real image, a lapse of time
that is sufficient to work it through entirely and render it in improved
form, ready to be digested. It is a gulf of temporary oblivion, a subtle
snare, a pass of the prestidigitator's hand. (LINDA would film our entire
journey through Crimea. I showed her how to do this with my cam-
corder, the latest model, complete with MEMORY BUFFER.)

"I want to show you how the instant camera works, too." (The
machine whirring in my hands.) "Look at this," I said, handing her
the shot. "Those are your legs." (LINDA's agile legs encased in jeans,
slender and rounded, much preferable to the sight of them unclad:
ugly prolongations of the torso finished off with feet, her toes joined
to each other by a membrane: *the mallard's webbed feet.*)

"Don't you think they're easier to see there, in the photo?"

I. "Stay, swift instant, you are so fair!" How difficult it is to put down
on paper the deep sorrow, the sad evocation of unhappy love, that a
song evokes when it moves us for a moment. It's always while we're
living, never while we're remembering the past, that we would like to be
conceded the grace of an eternal moment. We can't imagine that Goethe
uttered this phrase as he read an obscure poet of the Ming dynasty in the
solitude of his study. Only when we breathe happily beneath a blue sky
do we want to halt time, to withstand every one of its tiniest recesses.

But time's nature is inapprehensible; it remains deep in the background of our lives and, incapable of observing it objectively from the present moment, we know nothing, in the end, of its fierce transit. Only when we spend an idle moment leafing through old fashion magazines do we discover the degree to which that humanity, those others so different from ourselves, entered into contact with eternity. For the fashion that dictates a certain type of hairstyle—a feeling of well-being when attired in a made-to-measure suit, throatily *tra-la-la*-ing with all the exaltation of an opera singer, some tune from the last movie we saw—frees us from our fears about what was and what will be, to live in a perfect, orgiastic present.

a) In order to put past time—the old fashions—to the test, I have a scratched record with the songs I once enjoyed, a test-record. Each time I listen to it, there is, between today's "I" and the song that only yesterday filled me to my brim, an immense space, difficult to conceive of. The bass is no longer today's bass, so juicy, so pectoral; the highs are scandalously strident, the voices saccharine, the keyboards tinny. "What's missing here?" I wonder, displeased by this pallid music and the answer is: life is missing. Life, seasoned with the salt of *frivolity*, which is like the water we add to these dry, dehydrated songs to make them appetizing.

The idea of the past, the history of the universe, would be incomplete without this slight adjustment. The sensation of well-being—between sheets whose colorful patterns are designed to accord with the feeling of a today that already, by tomorrow, will be an embarrassing yesterday when it sees itself reflected with appalling fidelity in the photos of yesteryear and the collections of "oldies but goodies" advertised on the RADIO—is the principal motor of existence. Trivial, yes: but then life is, too.

Moon Walk. One afternoon we stopped at a pension in Yevpatoriya, beside the sea. As night fell, we strolled down to the little square with its dance floor where older couples, clearly VILLAGERS, circled slowly, as if they were herding the foreign rhythms that poured forth inexorably from the loudspeaker. I wanted to teach LINDA to dance and thus enable her to divine the beat's hidden accents without dispersing her energies in the cymbals' reverberation to smooth out the angles and display her skill at sketching the broader cadences that enclose the rhythm's less perceptible tremors.

In fact, for *P.O.A.*, it was enough that she could dance, whether or not she did it well. The important thing was to introduce a meaning into her moves, reproduce the process that had allowed me, during long dance sessions, to break down my *pas* into elemental gestures that might even be reduced to notations. One of these, in which I raised my arms to the height of my head and agitated them rhythmically as if saying good-bye, was indeed a good-bye to my former life full of worries, absurdly responsible, my sleepless nights. An innovative lighting technology of those years—a phantasmagorical strobe—immobilized the shuttlecock of my dancing into very crisp snapshots that emerged from the darkness one after another for as long as the blink of magnesium lasted. Beneath this light, interrogated by it, immobile in my own perception but actually in movement, I wondered one night: why do we dance? How to find a satisfactory explanation for this irrational fact? Was the world not full of inexplicable phenomena, then, if I couldn't find an answer to the question of something as trivial and widespread as dance? Incapable of sidestepping these lacunae in my knowledge, I found myself thinking of prehistoric shadows, totems, roaring lions, ritual cavorting around the bonfires. We kept on moving there, on that same dance floor, essentially as we did five or ten thousand years earlier, voguing freely across the savannah, a thing as elemental as the release of your breath. I was never again the same after that dance revelation.

Curiously, the only songs that aroused my enthusiasm were the *hits* of the moment. Very silly songs—Italian, mainly, in the mid-eighties— which, once the season was over, were cast off without an afterthought. The music didn't suffice unto itself, it was we who had to infuse it with life, connect it to our *up-to-date* nervous centers, surround it with the truths of the present day, season it with our acute awareness of our own youth and strength. We would stamp our feet in rage if some *disc jockey,* well intentioned but stupid, tried to stir us with a potpourri of old favorites; the revolutions of the dark mass of dancers would slow, as if encumbered by an invisible weight, a generalized yawning would ensue, people stumbling into each other, hisses. When we'd gone very limp, almost to the point of death, the *DJ* would inject us with a strong dose of some group that was very bad but very new, and we would hurl ourselves to the center of the floor once again and spend hours in a zone of time that could only be accessed through music and dancing: when their effect wore off, the grayness of your gray life awaited you.

MORRIS, WILLIAM. When, after nightfall, I sat on the terrace of the DACHA we'd rented in Crimea and devoted several hours to making some notes for this work, I would generally visualize myself as a Benedictine monk stooped over the *Imago Mundi* of Honorius Inclusus: the smoothness of the skillfully honed parchment, his miniaturized initials in blue and azure, the fine glints of gold leaf that he would study before printing this ENCYCLOPEDIA.

I. I would like to heighten the story of P.O.A. in some way, confer upon my book the status of those incunabula *in folio,* prized not for the apocryphal text they contain but for their beautiful illuminations depicting the garden of delights. I'll have to resort to the splendor of coated stock, perfect for photos in every color, like those magnificent ones of the Venice carnival I showed you; images that suggested to us the *essentially* different and more profound life led by Pierrots and Columbines. In the same way, this *Lexicon Universalis,* for which I've designed a cover with silver Cyrillic letters scattered chaotically across a field of blue—a composition that prefigures the eccentric character of the text, from which the reader can extract the title as from an *alphabet soup*—must be printed in accordance with the canons of an expensive fashion magazine. An entire fascicle with views of Saint Petersburg, pictures of you on every page, the multicolored Montgolfier that repeats the motif of those Russian cupolas in red, green, and blue; your delicate satin shoes in the foreground of the luxurious restaurant at the Astoria where we dined that night, and the PACKARD's chrome-plated grille, with its little stag, rampant . . . And since this, too, is now possible, I would insert perfumed strips impregnated with OPIUM, with Anaïs Anaïs, with the perfume in the multifaceted bottle I gave you that night in Fedosia, on the mountain.

A graphic solution that suggests the ephemeral life of the many books that will receive lukewarm reviews in the *Times Literary Supplement* this month, only to return, a week later, to their virtual existence in the depths of the computer, like deep-sea fish that appear on the surface for their brief hour then dive back down to be fed into the shredders where the unsold copies go. It wouldn't pain me if, once consulted, my ENCYCLOPEDIA were to be forgotten on the luggage rack of a commuter train. In fact, such a fate would be marvelously well suited to the philosophy underlying this ENCYCLOPEDIA. I would like for it to be sold at the magazine stands of the world's great train stations, where its resemblance to *Vogue* would confound the bored passenger: the *Harper's Bazaar* we find on a chair in the waiting room of an international airport that stays with us all the way to Capetown.

These are the multivalent graphic gems we will hand down to posterity. Essentially the same as those incunabula by Fiodorov, the first Russian typographer. In fact, when we get to Nice, I will personally take charge of the task of printing and binding it. Thirty copies to be given out to friends, as if it were a printed book and not a *manuscript*— a distinction that's about to disappear in our headlong return to the origins. It's very simple; my computer already has a fantastic arsenal of fonts.

II. As you already know, I disapprove of the text's independence from its material support. Though here, too, we're on the verge of going beyond—or rather, we've already left behind—the domain of printed paper. Let's think, rather, of one of those books printed on . . . No, better to say engraved with a laser on a photosensitive emulsion, the CD version of this same ENCYCLOPEDIA. (And of course its organization into *entries*, or *voces*, is no more than an old-fashioned mechanical simulation, on paper, of one of those new books available on CD.) Where does such a book begin, its beauty? In the fascinating litmus of a strange plaque we hold up to our eyes, seeking to discover beneath its mirroring surface, the signs, typefaces, and symbols we're accustomed to? For it contains a text we cannot manage to see, forms we do not succeed in imagining. Are these books, then? Can they be described as such? Where are the hard covers, the thin paper, the gilded edges, all the exquisite work of the Kelmscott *Chaucer,* the jewel designed by Morris that I promised to show you? I'll give you an example: do you believe that any trace of the hourglass can be detected in the pale green blink of seconds upon the liquid crystal? Books disappear the same way. We learn to rejoice in the lightness of the polyvinyl plaque, admiring its slenderness. Eventually we forget about the pleasing heft of coated paper.

N

NERUS (нерусь). "Young man," the duchess—every bit as xenophobic as Maarif—proffered in alarm, "you're quite mistaken!" Turning to me, after carefully removing the expression of complicity from her face, she added, "Forgive him. He doesn't know what he's saying."

But the pure falsity of her face belied her words; she hadn't gone to great effort to conceal the true feelings that surged within her, yet imagined she could deceive me by her clumsy maneuver, just as, controlling our rage with great difficulty, we attempt a smile and stroke the crew-cut head of a child, wanting all the while to give him a good slap. What had moved the duchess to intercede was like-mindedness. She pooh-poohed Maarif's accusations here, but would have proclaimed her adherence to them without a moment's hesitation if this were a street rally for the cause. These were ideas that must not be announced in the public realm before the time was ripe. "Pay no attention to him," she repeated, convinced, moreover, that I hadn't grasped even half of his peroration, which had been delivered *in Russian,* "the richest and most difficult language in the world."

Sometimes the anonymous housewives of whom the duchess reminded me would shout some instruction into your ear, which you understood perfectly the first time you heard it but opted, for whatever reason, not to carry out right away. Then they would say to each other, "I'm speaking to him *in Russian* and he doesn't understand me." Or else I might be talking with a friend in a public place and a woman, taking us perhaps for NERUS (non-Russians, representatives of one of the IMPERIUM's national minorities), would grow indignant: "Hey, why don't you speak *Russian?* You've been talking for half an hour in that twittering bird language of yours and it's making my head spin. You ought to be ashamed of yourselves." Then she'd get a better look at us and SPIT on the ground. "What can you expect from these NERUS?" The existence within the IMPERIUM of millions of NERUS who spoke other languages was ignored or barely tolerated. With the years and the advent of *The Fall of the House of [R]Usher,* I was witness to a traumatic mental transformation, an inversion of the magnetic poles of the *Rus,* now avid for a full and OCCIDENTAL life devoid of boiled potatoes or gherkins in brine.

NIGHTS, WHITE (Белые ночи). I shall now reveal the secret, the stupefying rabbit pulled from the hat, of the WHITE NIGHTS. The dimmed brilliance of the moon and sun at their equinox. I had expressly chosen the date, awaited the favorable conjunction of the stars, and though I've taken care not to mention what month we met in, the reader who knows the work of F.M. must have intuited by now that I wouldn't fail to take advantage of the phantasmagoric decor of the WHITE NIGHTS by describing a long walk through the insomniac city.

LINDA and I left the Astoria arm in arm. In the scant light of that hour, the colors of her dress and the scarlet of her lips were muted. I set my feet down very slowly as we walked, fighting against something I felt was about to spill open inside me and wash through my cranial cavity. When we reached the Ekaterinsky Canal, LINDA leaned her elbows on the parapet and watched, absorbed in the water's flow. After a while, she seemed to have come up with the words she'd been seeking for the previous half hour, even before the dispute with Maarif: "*Znaesh ne nuzhen mne tvoi roman. Ja dolzhna otkazatsia; ja peredumala. Maarif konechno prav.*"

It was like a bolt of lightning. Such a tirade, and delivered *in her very purest Russian:* "Know what? I've changed my mind. I'm not going along with your plan. Maarif is right." LINDA gave me no time to recover, to identify a tactic. She went on, "I can't seem to find anything in your plan that actually deserves a movement of my soul, an effort of my spirit. I will never be someone who thinks that fashion and dressing well—everything you talked about this afternoon in the garden—are anything to lose sleep over, or that can change my life. God knows, I understand perfectly that you were counting on my youth!"

"And on my money, LINDA!"

"And on your money, IOSIF. But do you think that's enough? You'd have to change me completely, make me into another girl. And I'm certain you wouldn't be able to do that. For us Russians there's no shame in being poor; on the contrary, the sin lies in riches. You can't imagine how remote all the wealth and ostentation you talk about is from my Russian soul."

When I heard that I breathed easier. She'd made a mistake. I hurried to take advantage of this opening.

"No, you Russians are essentially the same. It's just that you've forgotten. In 1915, more posters of La Kholodnaya were sold than photos of the Imperial family—which in my view is perfectly understandable. I'm only trying to teach you to hate certain things such as those horrible paintings by Dalí you picked out today. And Maarif's ridiculous Cossack overcoat, doesn't it make you laugh? You think it's a dumb joke, too, don't you?"

"But how can you pretend to know Russia? You, a foreigner? You'll never be able to. We're very different. You'll think I'm exaggerating, but I feel that the OCCIDENT has lost all its . . . sanctity? Yes, sanctity is the right word. Look, I haven't got a clear idea of where the failure lies, but I sense a certain false note in everything—a falsity that, in all sincerity, I don't find in the life we have in Russia. Perhaps, some day, we will become OCCIDENTALIZED, but without transforming ourselves internally. Anyway, you told me that what interests you is the nontranscendent, the trivial—but don't you want your novel to be transcendent? And what about the title? Not only does it include the word "soul," it's in Latin.[3] I perceive—and forgive me for telling you this—a profound contradiction between what you claim you want to do and your actual plan. Wouldn't irresponsibility and carelessness suit your novel better? Why this mania to record every detail of this summer?"

(This last argument struck a painful blow, I must acknowledge, and though I didn't consider it sufficient to invalidate my experiment on the spot, I haven't stopped thinking about it since.)

"The fact that I play the FLUTE, you know . . . And furthermore, there are personal reasons . . . There's my hamster . . . I have a hamster in a cage in my room. I wouldn't know who to ask to take care of him if I agreed to go on this trip with you."

"Maarif, maybe?" I hazarded in a whisper, dismayed by this unforeseen obstacle.

"Maarif!"—she laughed. "He would never be able to take care of a hamster. The poor thing would starve to death. He's not very practical. I must say that it was very intelligent of you to have chosen me, a woman, to consummate your plan. Maarif would never go along with such a project. And even I agreed to have dinner with you only out of curiosity. What harm could it do? Nothing could have been more innocent. But from there to accepting the whole story . . . No thanks. But really, everything was wonderful and you were terrific. Maarif!"

Which was to say: "Maarif, come on out of the shadows!" (I was perfectly well aware that he'd been following us.)

I. I was also perfectly well aware that it was Maarif who'd been speaking through her mouth. Now, as it happens, I also knew who had been speaking through Maarif's mouth. Her speech had contained an extremely important clue that cast her refusal in an entirely different light. She claimed to have no one to take care of her hamster, a dopey white-furred rodent, its cheeks perpetually stuffed with crackers. They sell hamsters in the *zoomagazini* along with Guinea pigs, little freshwater turtles, and goldfish. Another thing entirely is the entry that keeps company with "hamster" in the pages of the *Brockhaus and Efron Encyclopedic Dictionary* (Saint Petersburg, 1893). In Russian, hamster is хомяк (*khomiak*): dopey white-furred, *et cetera*. It's the entry which follows that sounds the note of alarm: Khomiakov, Alexei Stepanovich, hard-core Slavophile and author of two important treatises, *The Opinion of Foreigners about Russia* and *The Opinion of Russians about Foreigners*, from which Maarif, and now LINDA, had extracted the majority of the theses she had just shared. Two phantoms, two shadows, following us along the bank of that canal.

O

OCCIDENT, THE. The mirror in which Russia gazes at itself each morning to touch up its own image. A mental construct, a grandiose *civitas Dei* built on a foundation of weighty volumes *in folio,* bad films, and high-gloss consumer goods of widespread appeal, such as my BOO-GIE SHOES, to name but one example. Now, of course, seen from the IMPERIUM, the OCCIDENT presented a different aspect, as if it were a *levogyrate* or counterclockwise OCCIDENT. Viewed against a backdrop made not of steel but of polarizing glass. The inhabitants of the IM-PERIUM could distinguish Paris with their naked eyes, and a Parisian bistro and, seated at one of its little tables, a very manly bourgeois, none other than the very leftist writer Louis Aragon dipping his croissant into his coffee. On the table, to his *left,* the page proofs of *La Semaine Sainte.* This gentleman would raise an accusatory index finger, wrinkle his brow, give voice to irate discourses: these images were perceived with dazzling clarity. Their background could only be guessed at: dim shapes, zones of complete darkness where the eye could discern nothing beneath ink blots and the hysterical crosshatch of deletions. Occasionally, on very sunny days, floating torsos could be made out, which moved past disembodied legs, orphaned arms, and talking heads: the mutilated fauna of the OCCIDENT. Many suspected that these beings may once have had a human appearance, an integral existence, and desperately sought a position from which to make a closer study of them. A maneuver that would, for a second, allow them to make out shadows slipping through the superfine sieve of glass, shadows that declaimed at the top of their lungs, wielded paintbrushes, spun with dazzling skill on the tips of their toes—only to disappear back into the recesses of that unknown world.

I. Then, when at last one small volume of Borges—an Argentine writer and therefore suspect[4]—was published, a Russian friend of mine was assailed by the terrible suspicion that Borges was not Borges, but *one of the anthology's minor poets, a word in an index.* Since I came from the OCCIDENT, he brought his question to me: Was Borges no more than one of those narrow light sources that thus emerge from the trap of polarization, a weak ray that shone only in the IMPERIUM without being reflected in the rest of the world?

"A question that would have delighted Borges himself," was my first thought, and I did not concede much importance to the incident. But the next day, I, too, fell prey to a terrible doubt and hurried to consult *The Great Soviet Encyclopedia* (БСЭ, 1970 edition). To my astonishment, I found two entries under Borges, with identical Christian and surnames, one—"Borges, Jorge Luis: obscure, right-wing Argentine writer, a rigid formalist whose works are of little interest"—after the other, "Borges, Jorge Luis: son of Borisov, Georgi, emigrant from Rovno, naturalized in Argentina in 1863. A deeply learned man, author of profound works of literature who, nevertheless, has found little acceptance in an OCCIDENT scourged by formalist experimentation and who had to wait for translation into Russian before gaining millions of readers and the reception that his genius merits. A progressive thinker, he participates in the struggle of the Argentine people for total independence from England," *et cetera.*

OPIUM. The immense Volga and its tributaries, the gritty sand of its beaches, the boardwalks with their flower beds where no flowers grew and their bandstands for Sunday concerts by municipal orchestras were to any European capital what the actual fragrances of springtime, the sooty smell of river vapors, and the natural odors of a healthy and clean but human body were to OPIUM, the perfume Yves Saint Laurent launched that year.

The day had been warm and when night fell I strolled down to the city intending to take in some new release. I chose a seat on the last row of an almost empty cinema and spent an hour and a half on tenterhooks, ushered through the rings of cosmic dust that surrounded the inexplicable mystery of a crime, its spinning, floating mass suspended in space by forces we cannot comprehend, but there it is, we can touch it. And as I do so, I tremble from head to toe. Many summers have gone by since then and I think I may have lost this particular capacity. But that year I'd been reading tirelessly for months and was adjusted to react to the slightest stimuli: a very low threshold of response. It was easy for things to resonate deeply within me; I could be moved to tears by a story of loyalty, the hero who comes back years later and settles the score with a clean conscience. And I was much in need of pure essences, ideas uncontaminated by any hint of utilitarianism: abstract truths!

Halfway through the film, someone began vibrating a few yards away. Was it the spring climate or perhaps an emotion similar to mine? I sensed the emanations of an excellent perfume, undoubtedly French. Either it had taken half an hour to reach my nostrils or the singular emotion evoked by the film's mystery had opened new channels within me. I imagined her as a brunette; the scent was dark and rich. For a second, I weighed the possibility of attempting an approach on the way out of the cinema, but since we were in Muscovy I would risk encountering a sunny beauty with straight, blonde hair in a cloud of this perfume clearly intended for a dark-haired femme fatale—an apparently insignificant detail that might throw the entire experience off-kilter. I had learned to withdraw, had learned from Occam that essences must not be multiplied beyond what is necessary, and I went straight home.

I. Many years later, LINDA, the story continues. I happened to be in G**, a small city in the south of France, and discovered a *parfumerie*, the Nuit Napolitaine. A striped awning protected the lone flask in its window from the sun's rays and I leaned forward to get a closer look at the amber liquid within, the satin bow around the bottle's neck. A minute later, without having made any significant discovery, I adjusted my gaze to the mirrored surface of the glass and discovered my own eyes in the terrifying nearness of the reflection and, behind me, the specular image of this city where we are now, you and I—geraniums on the balconies, clean cobblestones, my bicycle leaning against a lamppost across the street. (I was in an excellent mood. Certain movies insist that we can achieve happiness by means of a twelve-speed bicycle and a baguette.)

But there remained a matter that had always puzzled me: the relationship between what was suggested by the name on the flacon and the fragrance of the perfume itself. I asked for a sample of that fragrance in the window and tried without success to capture some special meaning as I inhaled. Only an image of a barefoot young man in a very expensive suit walking along a dilapidated dock at a beach somewhere in the south: the advertisement that had launched this perfume on the market. Try as I might, I couldn't imagine anything but that old jetty, the reverberating sea. I had traveled to this city in search of fragrances that would be devoid of all reference, for perfumes are innately free of such things; it is we who, by christening them, endow them with a story, though we violate their *essential* vagueness when we attach names to them. In fact, we have no particular names for smells. We say "it smells like" and name the smell by analogy.

Scents thus introduce a terrifying *glissando* into our representation of the world: they are as invisible as sound, without limit of duration or spatial boundary. By giving names to perfumes, to fragrances, we seek to diminish this impression, to segment the continuum of smell into precise ideas that possess relevance and modernity. Now domesticated, these scents can establish a membrane between nature (this gray city, the dirty time of year) and ourselves: the cushion of air on which we glide, inaudible.

I was thinking of you, the red-haired girl I would choose for my novel, and wanted something clean and fresh. Monsieur Baldini, the shopkeeper, assured me he had what I was looking for. He went into the back and emerged with the last remaining bottle of a very old brand, sold out years ago, that contained no musk. When the bouquet of that antique treasure filled the air, I saw the uncontrollable mass spinning before me once more and felt the same emotion. How had this perfume reached the banks of the Volga? But of course it wasn't the same one. It was only the same base, without musk. Back in my hotel, I decanted this glass flacon, without a label, devoid of prehistory. Even I no longer remember its original name. I've thought of calling it LINDA. But your name, all on its own, would add nothing. I must unify these elemental lines into the complex organism of a publicity campaign and settle on its meaning, arbitrary but overflowing with emotion: the simple man who untangles the mystery of the girl's death, confronts the murderer, and kills him cleanly, not a muscle in his face even twitching, everything I felt that day in the darkened movie house. "Do you smell that fragrance? It's truly magnificent, it smells like you."

(First the striped awning, then the twelve-speed *mountain bike* pedaling along fast, a baguette sticking out of the saddle bag. Geraniums at the windows. France? The South of France? Night, the dark mass spinning in the void. A droplet falls onto LINDA's naked shoulder. *Fade out.*)

ORGANDY. The latest fashion is announced almost stealthily, a full season in advance; its manifestations are secondary and it moves out through the world as if traveling incognito. So that when, one day, from a moving car, we glimpse the striking feathery crest of a new hairstyle or see a winter scarf knotted around the neck like a cravat, we feel a start of discovery. Somewhat incredulous, we mentally review this vision until we are convinced. Yes, of course, what bliss: a narrow scarf knotted atop the overcoat collar as if it were a necktie, and in the course of the day we run into three, five fellow pedestrians, all tricked out like this, which is already an avalanche (because as soon as you notice the first manifestation, you're immediately amazed to discover how many people are already up-to-speed on the fashion). Which hasn't yet reached the circle of your most intimate friends and, therefore, when you arrive at that evening's gathering transformed into a dandy, one of them, the most absurd of the lot, the one most permanently deaf to all sartorial subtlety, asks you in amazement: "Huh? What's that necktie-scarf thingy? I don't like it at all, wouldn't be caught dead . . ." (and he's the one who, six months later, when no one else is doing it any more, goes on wearing his scarf that way for two more seasons). Later you doubt your own daring, wonder if perhaps you should wait a little longer and, on the way home, since it's very cold outside and you're afraid of catching flu, you wear the scarf in your usual manner. The next day, though, you go back to the more poetic style, the ends of your scarf flying in the wind.

(THELONIOUS was capable of mentally reproducing the evolution of the wristwatch from the massive oblong metallic rotundity so much in vogue at the beginning of the seventies to the superthin model of the mid-eighties. He visualized the process as if it were one of those educational films that show a sprout breaking through the shell of the seed and twirling up through layers of earth, continuing its ascent as a plant, turning to follow the path of the sun, losing its leaves, then disappearing, metamorphosed into pollen.)

I. With fabrics, with delicate ORGANDY, we can construct an ephemeral world of beauty. You must learn to distinguish the quality of a piece of cloth, its approximate value, at a glance.

I was sitting on the edge of the bed. LINDA passed in front of me and stepped out onto the balcony. The sea, its white foam. She had selected a string bikini that rode very high on the hips, but she seemed to notice something out there, the cypresses bent at a steep angle by a wind that was picking up, and she came back inside and changed into a lovely maillot, with real seashells sewn around the borders of the bust.

"A bathing suit is an abstraction, the smallest thing we can achieve with fabric," I explained to her. "These little snippets of cloth allow you to emerge from animality, they block the mammary glands, the physiological, from sight, and thereby diminish the horror of the naked body." LINDA was back out on the balcony, not listening.

". . . it represents the minimal effort of the human against the animal. Except that the wide straps of some of the older types of suits make them look a bit like underwear. That wouldn't suit you. It's the high chest that's in style, the line of the bust raised. Why don't you try on this pretty one-piece with a mesh back and a pattern of daisies and sunflowers. Except it makes you look even younger . . . Doesn't it amaze you how so few elements can transmit so many ideas? See what a fresh look those oversized buttons create! Okay, quite frankly, there's not much more I can say about swimsuits: I find Lycra a bit disconcerting, it repeats the naked body in some way. What do you think about wrapping this delicate length of ORGANDY around the hips?

It will lift the ensemble a little, your legs showing through the transparency, their fierce line . . ."

Finally LINDA was standing in front of the mirror trying on a little pea green hat.

"How's this?"

"Look at that . . . It's amazing! That ORGANDY wrap can be even more interesting than a dress. But the shoes, LINDA! What shoes will you wear down to the beach? I'd completely forgotten about that. There's nothing more difficult than choosing a pair of shoes for a swimsuit. If you wear that pair with high heels, I won't be able to look at you when you walk along the path ahead of me. It disturbs me to see women dressed that way, far too approachable and defenseless, as if they were open to an activity considerably more intimate than a stroll. If you go barefoot, though, your walk will be somnambulant, arduous, and the slow dance of the ORGANDY wrap will only heighten that impression. Try that nice pair of sandals we bought in Saint Petersburg, just before setting out on our trip. You've worn them all too often since then, but I can't think of anything better."

P

PACKARD. I suspect that we are, to our Creator, as complex and mysteriously distant as machines, and that he swells with pride when he observes our perfection. In much the same way, we are unaware of the laws that govern the aesthetic evolution of the automobile; how it ceased to be the imperfect replica of a horse-drawn carriage and instead blossomed into the dazzling curves of the postwar PACKARD. Neither do we understand the first thing about the incurable malaise that has attacked the motor vehicles of today, the causes of the regression that makes them more alien and horrible to look upon each year. It is torture to watch how designers—perhaps perturbed by the idea of the archetypal auto, the *mobilis*—have gradually stripped them of mudguards, running boards, chrome diadems, nickel-plated hubcaps; how, trapped in a vortex of perpetual transformation, they've veered in the wrong direction toward functionalism, aerodynamics, an absurd notion of comfort. It requires a great effort to understand this, for we never imagine that a hundred years of evolution could be enough to exhaust a set of forms; we continue to believe that thousands of different models, with new protuberances, await us—but that is not the case. The thesis of lineal progress ad infinitum denies what we know about the spiral of development with its declines and recoveries. And it's clear that we now find ourselves at the end of a phase, LINDA, very far from the decade of true splendor to which this PACKARD belongs. You can't imagine how much work it was to find it. You Russians have nothing from this period; the entire stratum is empty, nary a molar nor an occipital bone pitted with holes: nothing. This model is from '49 (the straight-eight engine, three speeds, maximum velocity ninety-five miles per hour) and I'll have you know that according to the crook at the rental agency this car once belonged to Beria, the fearsome Minister of the Interior. Ah, yes, the inevitable mythic provenance that adds 15 percent to the price. I didn't hesitate to pay, the very latest fashion in cars is to prefer these beautiful models from the forties, built for an efficient drive, conscientiously prepared for the road like those elderly couples, tourist fossils from the BADEN-BADEN era, who buy pith helmets, binoculars inlaid with mother-of-pearl, a rattan basket for provisions, a cashmere throw against the evening chill, sunglasses with tortoiseshell frames. A lost precision: the visible evidence of expenditure. When I was a boy I'd help my grandfather wax his Oldsmobile and shine its nickel-plated grille. Then we'd go for a ride, simply to enjoy the pleasure of speed: the tufted leather upholstery, the steering wheel's imitation-bone Bakelite. I would sit very close to him, not wanting to miss any part of the way he yanked the stick shift and slammed on the clutch. Alongside us were Pontiacs and the omnipresent Chevrolets, the couples within them embracing as if they were relaxing on an enormous sofa, Paul Anka blasting from the RADIO . . . How to explain this to you?

I know you would have preferred one of those modern cars from Japan. I've learned to hate them. Japan is nothing but a parvenu in the OCCIDENTAL work of machinery, a clever imitator, incapable of capturing the profound logic that underlies the four speeds of the internal combustion engine. Have you ever seen a Japanese oil painting? It's the same thing. The coloring is sickly, the composition chaotic, the touch of the brush uncertain. Where automobiles are concerned, they haven't been able to come up with an equivalent to the fine technique of an Utamaro, a Suzuki Harunobu, those exquisite woodblock prints on rice paper. Only the Chinese, far wiser, have discovered the crowd of cyclists, the hybrid rickshaw. Isn't the apparent ease with which a cyclist pedals, though all his muscles are straining, more Oriental? As is the modest size of the sedan chair. But this tendency toward lightness, when translated into automobile design, brought on the disaster of the horrible Nissan, the irresponsible airiness of the Mazda. The Japanese invasion has been successful because it found an important chink in the OCCIDENTAL bloc: the aerodynamic tendency. Evidence of which can be found in the showy "ducktail"—you see? Flight!—at the beginning of the sixties. Then in the seventies the Arabs had us worrying about not using so much oil, which meant we were ready when Ford, in despair, launched its execrable Torino, an entirely plain vehicle, nothing at all for the imagination to cling to, antiseptic.

I'm comforted only by the knowledge that vehicles propelled by solar batteries are on their way, and these new ecological cars, these *ʒen* cars—their retractable headlights making them look like insects—may give rise to automobiles that are fundamentally new, perhaps in no way different from arachnids, a complete fusion with nature: an emergence from the kingdom of the machine into something else. Can't we view the horse as the final phase of the prehistoric automobile that belonged to the civilization prior to ours? Isn't it true that the Japanese—them again!—have invented a many-limbed robot, the prototype of some future means of transport?

(We drove toward the sea together across the coastal hills, our PACK-ARD swift and ultrapowerful; LINDA eating her fill of grapes for the first time in years. The vineyards of Crimea.)

PALACE (CHINESE). I got off the train at O**, near Petersburg, at the beginning of June. The station virtually a ruin. Birdcalls in the silence, a warm breeze. To judge by the scant number of passengers continuing on, there must have been only two or three more stops on the line. At the edge of a shady grove of oak trees I came to a fence that bore the map of the park. I studied it as if it were an animated tableau and I a medieval knight confronting the thousand possible paths across a game board that chance might dictate. My finger inexorably traced the route to the CHINESE PALACE. I was thirsty. Birdcalls in the silence, a warm breeze.

How could I have imagined that what awaited me around a bend in that hedge maze would turn out to be an unexpected augury of the sort provided by the *I Ching*? The CHINESE PALACE was not the Ming pagoda, the gilded pavilion I had imagined. For a moment I thought I'd lost my way and had reached some imperial DACHA of Peter III heretofore unsuspected by historians. A pond—a small artificial lake with ducks—reflected the Italianate volutes of a PALACE entirely devoid of Asiatic complexities. I consulted the sign to be certain I hadn't made a mistake. The caption, as revealing as a conceptualist label, read: CHINESE PALACE. And since, effectively, this Russian PALACE was thus transformed into the CHINESE PALACE I was seeking, I thought of two more plaques. One in front of the lake that read *Sea*, and the other over the little house for the ducks, stating *Gryphons*.

I found the basket of slippers for visitors entirely at my disposal; the season had only just begun. I chose a shapeless green pair with elastic bands at the heels then stood up and walked forward uncertainly, a centimeter of felt between the soles of my feet and the floor. As I waited for the guide, it began to rain. There would be no other visitors today. I crossed the threshold and shuffled along with difficulty, giving the parquet floor a nice polish, and for free.

The guide, a shawl draped over her shoulders, had the tired face of a schoolmistress prepared to repeat a boring lesson about anaerobic respiration, a subject that escapes both her comprehension and her immediate perception. Her palaver followed a strict rhythm and bothered me as an inopportune fog would have, or rather, a light that was overly bright. Facing a writing desk with mother-of-pearl inlay, I intensified my scrutiny in an attempt to elude her explanations (date of manufacture, provenance) and, leaning forward to observe its delicate iridescence more closely, understood, suddenly, that the owner of that PALACE had also tried to free himself from a boring European existence (which must have annoyed him as much as the guide's aimless blather was irritating me) by surrounding himself with Chinoiseries. There in the left wing of his PALACE, he could embark on excursions into the virtual cosmos of a life exempt from fatiguing service to Mother Russia. He had accumulated bronzes and porcelains, spheres of carved openwork marble, carpets showing the crane of wisdom and the tortoise of longevity, as if he were never going to die, which is the illusion of those who exist in the perfect present moment of their knickknacks.

It was an ideal PALACE to live in, with minimal distance between my bosom and its magnificence. It made you feel that its owner, the gentleman who loved Japanese lacquers, had gone out for a brief stroll in the garden and would return, from one moment to the next, to the steaming samovar, afternoon TEA almost ready. The very fact that the Germans hadn't occupied it during the war—information provided by the guide—lent it the attraction of goods prudently placed in the vault of a Swiss bank, safe from any danger.

I was incapable of imagining myself CZAR of all Russia, lord of the Grand Duchy of Muscovy, summering in Petergoff. But the CHINESE PALACE could well have been mine, along with a pair of thoroughbreds and its collection of Chinoiseries. To stroll through its rooms was to tighten and pluck the strings of many readings and images that had hung loosely in my thoracic cavity until then. They'd been dangling there for years, occasionally emitting beautiful notes, but the process by which they were tuned at last culminated in that PALACE and left me ready to be played upon by the long fingers of stimuli that were essentially insignificant.

But equivalent, I hasten to clarify. Only years later did I have the money to begin overcoming, little by little, in tiny baby steps, the cosmic distance that separated me from a life such as that one. It was like throwing *things* into an unfathomable abyss—$2 million mansions, fifty-five-meter yachts, holidays in Oceania—never, in any case, to achieve any diminution of the gap. Yet this could cause me no pain. The man who is born owning a golf course never comes to understand the formidable pressure, the truly fundamental value of such a possession. I, in effect, had nothing, absolutely nothing; however, like a bronzed torso in an advertisement, I had *captured the spirit*. To caress the jade of the little statues was to touch the curving limb of the crane in flight, offered by the Zen master but invisible to my blind eyes. Or it was as if the spirit of the owner of the PALACE had appeared in the flesh before me to break his walking stick over my shaven head.

I tossed the slippers into their basket, looked out at the garden through the graph of the windowpanes and saw that the sun was shining again over the lake and its ducks. Here was the beautiful backdrop to another mise en scène, the brief appearance of a character who would play an extremely important role in my initiation.

I. From the far end of the set, emerging from the depths of the park, I saw the white blur of a summer dress approaching. I quickly abandoned the foyer and went into the garden to intercept her at the little duck house. Sixteen or seventeen years old, to judge by her schoolgirl air. She wore a pair of comfortable leather sandals and let me accompany her without giving an instant's thought to the emptiness of the park, the clumps of shrubbery, the humidity of the hour. Intrepidity, vigor, a walk that placed all her weight on the sole of the foot. By the time we reached the road that led back to the train station we'd already talked quite a bit and she'd allowed me to run my hand over her hair which was the color of burnished bronze. At that moment, standing there at the crossroads, I discovered that she wasn't wearing a dress, as I'd thought, but a skirt and blouse in the same color.

Our train departed from N**, only two stops farther in the opposite direction, at 6:35. It would arrive in fifty minutes. In the station restaurant, we asked for mushroom soup and toast. We ignored the kebab platter that, I now realize, cost almost nothing. The soup turned out to be wonderful; there was excellent cooking to be had in Muscovy in those days. Then we spent a long time talking. She showed me a notebook full of writing. She had jotted down the family names of the Italian architects, the cost of the restoration, the time it would take to complete. Minutes before the train arrived, we each paid our own check, a ruble and some kopecks, without the slightest embarrassment. We continued our chat onboard: a marvel of a woman (I'm trying to paint her portrait here). I'd admired the sheen of her hair. We had conversed. It was an experience. We said good-bye without exchanging addresses or arranging to meet again. It would have been a mistake on my part to consider her anything more than a *sign,* easy on the eyes, muse-worthy. I'd succeeded in becoming a lad equipped for something more than reading books.

PANIS ORIS INTUS ANIMAE MEAE (P.O.A. *or* BREAD FOR THE MOUTH OF MY SOUL). Yes, I wanted to write a great novel, but one that was based on insignificant feelings, the dot matrix of my existence, the pettiness of consumerism and OCCIDENTAL flotsam and jetsam, the indispensable bauble of each new day. I dreamed of repeating the success of those composers of RADIO hits who move us to tears with a melody that is cheap and cloying but deeply felt. I yearned to capture an era, that summer, all that was destined to vanish without leaving a trace, to be forgotten, just as we lost the Philadelphia rhythms of my teenage years. Who would write about that? This was my primordial goal: to freeze the vertiginous shifts in the external attributes of human life, that great immobile organism, inalterable in its gross corpulence, which takes childish delight in transforming its attire, like a mime who, during a single performance, quick-changes between Harlequin, Polichinelle, and Cantonese Mandarin costumes. For that's what we do: betray the old fashions to make a show or pretense that we are living. Or rather, in fact, to live *precisely* that fatuity. I had decided to return to Saint Petersburg to *live* BREAD FOR THE MOUTH OF MY SOUL, to model my discovery about *frivolity* onto the surface of the real world and study the influence of FLUORIDE on a young soul (a Russian soul). That the girl I would finally select played the FLUTE fit miraculously into my plan due to the widespread stereotype about Russians and classical music *et cetera.* I'd come up with the title years earlier, a phrase from Saint Augustine's *Confessions,* PAN DE LA BOCA DE MI ALMA, which explained the sensation similar to hunger that I felt on seeing certain shades of red. I visualized this inner MOUTH OF MY SOUL as a moist purple hole opening crosswise in the region of the solar plexus, ravenous as a baby bird in its nest. To sate it, I had to shovel in all the tactile, visual, and auditory stimuli available: a woman friend's clean skin, K**'s delicate shoulders and deep anatomical hollows, the perfect design of my fountain pen, THELONIOUS's vertiginous fingers on BRILLIANT CORNERS, that perfect piece of music, warm and pliant.

I. The name of THELONIOUS would remain in the memory of generations to come, like that of Casanova de Seingalt[5] who visited Saint Petersburg in 1764. A fragment of his *Memoirs,* which I consulted before undertaking my own journey, struck me as premonitory. Casanova says:

*M'étant ecarté de la maison impériale d'une centaine de pas, je décou-
vris une jeune paysanne dont la beauté était surprenante. L'ayant fait
remarquer au jeune officier, nous nous acheminâmes vers elle; mais,
leste et svelte comme une biche, elle s'enfuit jusqu'à une chaumière
peu éloignée, où elle entra. Nous l'y suivons . . .*

*Sa gorge n'était pas encore parfaitement développée, car elle avait
à peine quatorze ans. Blanche comme la neige, elle avait des cheveux
d'ébène d'une longueur et d'une épaisseur prodigieuses. Deux arcs
d'une extrême perfection et d'une grande finesse recouvraient deux
yeux admirablement fendus, qu'on aurait pu désirer un peu plus
grands peut-être, mais qu'on ne saurait imaginer ni plus brillants,
ni plus expressifs.*

*Cette jeune fille, que je baptisai [Zizi], monta en voiture et
nous suivit à Pétersbourg vêtue de gros drap et sans chemise. Je
m'enfermai quatre jours, sans la quitter un instant, jusqu'à ce que
je la vis habillée à la française, sans luxe, mais très proprement.*

Or: *I was about a hundred paces from the imperial residence when I
saw an enchanting young peasant girl. I pointed her out to my friend
and we walked toward her, but she ran away, light and graceful as a
gazelle, into a sad little hut. We followed her inside . . .*

*Her breasts were not yet completely formed; she had just turned
fourteen. Her snow-white skin contrasted with her thick ebony hair.
Her fine black eyebrows rose over a pair of magnificently shaped
eyes that I would have preferred a little larger, but that seemed to
shoot out flames. I must also mention her teeth, made for kisses . . . I
christened her [ZIZI] and she got into the carriage and returned with
us to St. Petersburg dressed in coarse clothes, without a chemise of
any kind . . . For four days I stayed home, never leaving her until I
had dressed her modestly in the French style.*

II. A few notes for P.O.A.

[1]*At the end of the summer we'll take a trip to* YALTA. It was the old dream of a vacation in Hawaii. Yes, some readjustment of scale was required, but that couldn't change the significance of the journey or of the sea in our lives. The Crimean coastline, the antique resonance of its city's names—Feodosiya, Livadia, Yevpatoria—suited my project perfectly. The beaches, the sea, symbolized freedom in the abstract, connoted laxity, luminosity, the diaphanous air filling our lungs. Then, if my experiment turned out to be successful, we would travel to the real Riviera, which, for me, was also Fitzgerald's *Tender is the Night*.

[2]*Winged lions.* The medieval bestiary known as the Physiologus tells us that the winged lion is the symbol of the EVANGELISTS, who are often represented as the lion of Saint Mark or the bull of Saint Luke, as well. A happy coincidence. When I was location-scouting for PANIS ORIS INTUS ANIMAE MEAE, I'd chosen the lovely bridge that spans the Griboedev Canal, a few meters from Nevsky Prospekt. From there, one of the most beautiful views of Saint Petersburg opens out before your eyes.

[3]*And what about the title? Not only does it include the word "soul," it's even in Latin.* ANIMAE or "soul" was a concept as readily mass-produced as any other. Everything acquired another life within the easy world of *now*. I could make Saint Augustine a hero of *frivolous* culture, transform BREAD FOR THE MOUTH OF MY SOUL into a terrific marketing slogan, magnifying the story of his renunciation of paganism (the mirror image of my own conversion to the idolatry of the present) and taking his *Confessions* along with me to the top of the best-seller lists by publishing this ENCYCLOPEDIA to coincide with the launch of P.O.A.: a triple-decker cheeseburger. Obviously it wouldn't be enough for my book simply to tell the truth about *frivolity;* I would also have to mint the idea anew, render it accessible, transform it into some gesture

or characteristic that would make it easily and positively identifiable, a topic of fashionable conversation during TEA time.

[4] . . . *Borges, an Argentine writer, and therefore suspect.* Quite surprisingly, I was Cuban. This earned me accusations of being a PSEUDO DEMETRIUS, an imposter. How could I pretend to represent the rich OCCIDENT? While this seemed a valid objection, it was, in fact, a serious error. An entirely OCCIDENTAL man, if such a thing exists, would never have discovered the important role that *frivolity* had played in discrediting the Doctrine, would not have perceived the ravages wreaked by FLUORIDE upon the old Russian soul. My adolescence spent in an *essentially frivolous* country, but one that had placed all its bets on the seriousness of the Doctrine, had endowed me with perfect mastery of the casuistries that an in-depth analysis of the phenomenon required. For on more than one occasion, fearful of having been contaminated, I had knelt to make my confession before the barred window of my own conscience and found myself *full of love* for (SWISS) CHOCOLATES. What I mean is that I'd never taken my eyes off that other side of life, even when I was bound hand and foot, and this dual existence had, over time, contributed to my discovery.

[5] . . . *Casanova de Seingalt.* The author of the *Nights of Saint Petersburg,* Joseph-Marie, comte de Maistre, must also be mentioned here, if only for the coincidence of José(ph): JOSIK, JOSHELE, JOSEPH. (Russia had been waiting for me to introduce its citizens to the elaborate structures of my island's literature. I'd lived long winters in its very heart, like Bowles in Tangiers: the desolate snow, the age-old despair of the dunes.)

PASARELA (*or* CATWALK). Here's the final speech I managed to deliver on the roof of our hotel in YALTA, as filmed by LINDA. A very slow pan takes in the depth of the sky, a flotilla of cirrus riding out over the sea. A serene introductory moment, flooded with light, for by then we believed the danger was past and we were safe from the jaws of the ravenous pack, the bolt securely drawn.

I watch myself balance along the edge of the roof and come to a halt. With my back to LINDA, I study the landscape, the beauty of the view that expands in my lungs. I turn to the camera, arm extended, and say something we cannot hear, the beginning of a last discourse of farewell to the summer, the beautiful view, the play of shadows at twilight, words that fall into the void and die without being registered, because of some defect in the camera or some carelessness on the part of LINDA, who may have neglected to engage the sound button, I will never know.

It was my last lecture of the summer. I don't recall a single point I made in this "presentation," which now, owing to its muteness, has taken on far greater force than all the others I delivered that summer for—as I'd explained to LINDA—the truly wise teacher "preaches the doctrine without words." I began with a broad circumlocution, addressing—or so it would appear—general definitions: the sun on the line of the horizon, the blue sea, the vastness my open arms sought to embrace. Then, rejecting the vague imprecision of the landscape, the natural order, my right hand sketched a circle of light around myself, the contour of the soles of my feet, my personal world. With my palm turned upward, fingers wide, I reviewed my clothing, the impeccable crease of my pants, the thick silk tie. This resplendent attire clearly demonstrated the immense sense of well-being that could be extracted from the neutral material of a few bodies, a summer like any other. I gave signs of satisfaction. My lips pronounced a single word three or four times, a word that, when I first watched the video, I couldn't decipher. Until it dawned on me that I was speaking in Russian. Then I understood: "Хорошо!" "*Horosho! Horosho!*" ("Good! Perfect!")

An affirmation followed by an ample parenthesis of my hands, my fingers, touching each other at the pads, outlining the shape of a narrow cell, the slope of a roof. My brows respond with astonishment, I close my eyes . . . my mouth emits sounds of indignation with particular emphasis on the letters *o* and *ʒ*. I speak without pausing for breath (now seated on the parapet). The bleary look in my eyes betrays the fact that I am on the verge of a serious bout of blindness. During a pause I see myself raise my head and rub my temples desperately, my eyesight gone. Very little illumination reaches the rooftop by now, only the oblique light of a sun slowly sinking. The white blur that is my shirtfront appears at evenly spaced intervals when I lean forward to underscore a phrase or stretch my chin away from my throat so that my words—highly profound sentences, important conclusions—can reach LINDA on the opposite parapet, from where she is filming me. The light's fluctuation now seems rhythmic, imbued with unmistakable significance, and at a given moment it speeds up as if announcing the imminent advent of the tragedy, endowing the scene that will soon erupt with its desperate tempo.

My face undergoes an earthquake: I give a start, one, two, three times as the air transports the vibrations of a hail of kicks against the trapdoor. RUDI's men have taken a long time to appear, but here they are, come to attack me and steal all my money. I stand and walk toward the camera but LINDA pans away for a second and we see the trapdoor jumping. Then comes the eruption, a black substance spewing forth. Five portions of magma, all in a state of inexplicable fury.

Then I reappear standing on the parapet. I slap my chest and let out a yell I have no trouble deciphering. "Over here, RUDI!" A move designed to distract him from LINDA. I pick up the bouquet of carnations and walk away, balancing along the narrow wall. Then I turn and offer the thugs a scowl of deepest disdain. I extend my right hand and hang a text in the air (as in one of La Khalodnaya's silent films), a text that shines white against the deep blue of the sky: "One more step and I'll jump!" These five little men (one of them wielding an AX) stop in their tracks, terrified: my suicide would greatly complicate their flight across the snowy mountains of the Caucasus. While their surprise lasts, I pretend to weigh my options and, finally, make a gesture of reconciliation: "We could reach an agreement, *gospada*." I lower my eyes, arrange my face in an expression of resignation, and slowly take out my wallet. I make a show of counting the amount of our costly ransom, but suddenly straighten triumphantly, fling all my credit cards at them and shout: "No cash at all, *muchachos*." Which I followed with a gale of Homeric laughter, a final ray of sun glinting against the barrier of my teeth.

Now I can confess: I'd decided to die, put an end to the suffering caused by seeing so *deeply*, having so full an awareness of the unbearable beauty of the world. I'd managed to conceal from LINDA the constant attacks of my malady, when the world fell apart into gems and quartzes whose BRILLIANT CORNERS I studied, entranced and blinded by their gleam. And now, on this rooftop, it no longer mattered to me whether I died, whether I threw myself into the abyss like a Hyperborean (see EURASIA, Pliny's notes) committing suicide after a life of excess. Neither the success of my experiment nor the love that, I could almost swear, I'd been able to awaken in LINDA, had managed to calm my despair, alleviate my fleshly existence, halt the course of my sickness. There, at the edge of the parapet, two steps away from the ravenous pack that was gaping at my credit cards without yet understanding a thing, I turned to LINDA to say good-bye. I see myself raising my eyes, seeking some motive that will explain my decision, pointing my index finger toward the sky, opening my mouth to emit a first phrase—the all-important fact, the new line of discourse we decide to embark on when we suddenly realize we've wasted two-thirds of the allotted time, and we organize our thoughts, take a deep breath, the central thesis blazing in our mind—"Listen, LINDA, the notion . . ." and then I begin to blur, affected by an actual earthquake, furrows of fire that shoot across my face: LINDA, who at that moment throws down the camera and bolts for the trapdoor. Apparently, the fall activated the sound button. It's the last thing the camera recorded: my image, vanishing, and a cry that now fills me with joy and sadness: "THELONIOUS, jump!"

(The real world is naught but appearance. If we continue to have some sort of objective existence when our eyes are closed it's only because we're imagined by a being, a BOGATYR, asleep outstretched in a field, head resting on a hummock. He is the last bastion, the final dream that contains us all. LINDA's cry, almost a scream, made him crack open an eye, blink for a second, and then o dark dark dark they all go into the dark: me, LINDA, RUDI, YALTA, Russia, immensity itself, all go into the dark.)

PETER I (пэтэр I). The tyrant indispensible to Muscovy's enormity. A man of wide-ranging temperament—a Russian—he spent several years as an apprentice carpenter in Zealand, caulking the Russian Navy's first ships. His indisputable talent earns him the same indulgent treatment as the drunken master craftsmen who plague the IMPERIUM's factories: he's accepted as an irremediable affliction, "very much our own." Saint Petersburg, for example, the resplendent Germanic city he founded on the unhealthy and shifting delta of the Neva, стоит на костях (*stoit na kostiah*), that is, *took root upon the bones* of many thousands of Russian muzhiks. Figuratively, of course: but when I heard this terrible accusation for the first time I thought PETER had given the order to fill in the delta's sandbanks with the corpses of the builders—the technique used by the Ch'in for the Great Wall.

But PETER is credited with an even more horrendous crime: that of having introduced the discordant note of the batiste handkerchief into the simple world of the boyar caftan. For this daring and premeditated attack against the patriarchal order of the Grand Duchy of Muscovy, he would never be completely forgiven. A life-size sculpture of him done in wax is on display in the Hermitage: a man of great stature, he rises high on narrow calves, *stoit na kostiah*. He's dressed in the cosmopolitan garb he brought back from his trip to Europe: the scandalous square-toed Dutch shoes with buckled arches and heels of painted wood (no more of those Asiatic buskins with the tips of the toes curling back!); his skinny tibia clad in stockings, matador-style, held up by a simple garter; close-fitting breeches of blue wool; the bow tie of fine silk; and the brocade frock coat adorned with a double row of buttons (no more of those caftans reaching all the way to the floor!); a sparse beard; a small and impertinent mustache; and, finally, a tricorne (no more of those floppy woolen caps!) atop a wig of powdered curls.

One winter afternoon in 198* I visited the pantheon of the Romanov family in the cathedral that stands within the walls of the Peter and Paul Fortress. I was accompanied by T**, a friend, who had insisted on showing me PETER's sepulchre. Frozen stiff, our hats pulled down on our heads, we approached a group that was receiving the usual litany from a guide's lips: PETER I, the good CZAR who founded a city, distributed land and organized the Russian army . . . When he reached the point of the city built *na kostiah* . . . I, who was hearing the story for the first time, was horrified and sought clarification of this turn of phrase—figurative or literal?—from my friend. Our whispers caught the guide's attention and he lifted his head (which had been downcast by the useless sacrifice of thousands of Russian souls) and detected ours, with hats on. Then, without preamble or introductory note, like a sports car going from zero to ninety-five kilometers an hour in the span of ten meters, he thrust his sacerdotal index finger at us: "They haven't bared their heads before PETER!" and waited for everyone to turn and look before repeating with a hiss: "They haven't bared their heads before PETER!"

Then he stared at me and proffered from between clenched teeth: "NERUS! What can we expect from a NERUS." This statement entirely overlooked the fact that PETER I had reigned over an IMPERIUM that included millions of NERUS, even as it affirmed the immortality of PETER I, the only surviving CZAR.

PSEUDO DEMETRIUS. In Russian, for "imposter," they (we) have the word самозванец, *samozvanets*, "he who gives a name to himself," a very conceptualist idea, we'd say today. In 1602, PSEUDO DEMETRIUS revealed himself to the monks of the Kiev Pechersk Lavra as the CZAREVITCH Dimitri, son of Ivan the Terrible, believed to have been murdered on Boris Godunov's orders. He pushed back the hood of his habit, stabbed his index finger at his chest, and gave himself a name. But his "sheep's eyes" ran in despair across the vast field of his face and the monks expelled him willy-nilly. When the figure of Grigory Otrepyev was no more than a distant point far down the Dnieper river, the prior SPAT in rage and baptized him without needing to consult the book of saints: *imposter*.

Neither beard nor mustache grew on Grigory's face. He was small in stature, disproportionately broad of shoulder, and short of neck. He was, moreover, five years older than the CZAREVITCH, who was, in fact, murdered in Uglich. Nor did he suffer from epilepsy, and, as we've seen already, he had to struggle grimly against a physiognomy that often betrayed him. The only things that distinguished him were his beautiful CALLIGRAPHIC handwriting and his undoubted talent as a con artist, for he had discovered a gold mine, a vacant niche in the pantheon of Russian gods.

Mortal enemy of mirrors, he marches to Poland, where God himself places in his path a beauty, Marina Mniszech, who comes to close the circle: beauty and the beast. (I've invented nothing here; this is the most astonishing story I heard in Russia!) While we do not know with certainty how he managed to win her favor, it would appear that she yielded to a promise that overran the narrow limits of a Polish maiden's imagination: "You shall be empress of Russia." A truly powerful oath; any woman would have lost her head. (Two centuries later, even Catherine the Great, on the night of the coup d'etat that brought her to the throne—the soft thump of the pillow over the mouth of the sleeping Peter III—paced nervously until dawn. When at last she was informed of the operation's success, the news would turn out to be somewhat imprecise, for it omitted the corollary that from Peter III's still-warm body the ethereal copy of an *imposter* had detached itself, as in a Disney cartoon, leapt into the garden, and spurred its steed away: two ghosts, rider and steed, to whom Catherine would never give chase.)

Grigory, the *samozvanets*, embraces the Catholic faith and thus obtains the support of King Sigismund III and the Knights of the Teutonic Order. When he crosses the border into Muscovy, Grigory is weaving, day and night, the delicate fabric of a correspondence composed in his painstaking copyist's CALLIGRAPHY. Epistles that projected over the snows of the north, the forests, and the STEPPE, the austere gaze, the lofty brow, the energetic chin of a CZAR who, without firing a single blunderbuss, without so much as a clash of spears, entered victoriously into Moscow, the third Rome.

When Gudonov's *strelitzi* stormed the Kremlin eleven months later, PSEUDO DEMETRIUS had already drunk deep of the true loveliness of Marina, the beautiful. (I don't know whether it's due to this that Polish women even today enjoy an inalterable reputation as great beauties: писаные красавицы.) My sources shed no light on the final destiny of the woman who was, without the shadow of a doubt, the most beautiful CZARINA of Muscovy. (Catherine the Great, née Catherine Anhalt-Zerbst, was a thickset German *frau*.)

On May 16, at dawn, PSEUDO DEMETRIUS, like a quick-change artist fleeing from a burning theater, flung his CZAR mask to the floor and fled in terror down the Kremlin's long passageways, the redness of his face *in crescendo*. Cornered in a hallway in the north wing, he breaks down the heavy shutters with a kick of his rose-colored buskin and thinks of the contrast between the hard oak boards and Marina Mniszech's white breasts. Then he jumps—his once unfathomable credit in the coffers of good luck now reduced to zero—and idiotically dislocates his ankle. Forty-eight hours of life remain to him, enough time for him to be chained, burned alive as an example, and have his ashes stuffed into a cannon with an equal measure of gunpowder: the thundering salvo . . . Over the course of the following year, the cloud that emerged from the cannon's mouth traveled all the way around the globe to precipitate once more, in the summer of 1607, into the human mold of PSEUDO DEMETRIUS II, atomically identical, the next chapter in the interminable history.

R

RADIO TORTURE. I'm visiting a friend's home for the first time. I ring the doorbell (there are many different types of doorbell in the IMPERIUM: chirping birds, a concierge's squawk, *do-re-mi* chimes—any of those). Inside, I'm given a very cordial welcome. There's talk of a two-week stay, a month if necessary. That night we stay up late conversing and I go to bed dead tired. At six the next morning, an announcer's thunderous voice brusquely drags me from an apolitical dream and, with my soul in an uneasy state of suspension, I become aware of the successes of the industrial production sector in Western Ukraine followed by various other industrial feats achieved in the region of the Sea of Japan, then hear a summary of the international news followed by a men's chorus from Georgia. They must have forgotten to turn the RADIO off last night, I think. At eight—having missed two hours of much-needed sleep—I am nevertheless tense, ready to form ranks, and fully aware of what is going on in the world.

The pressure exerted by these devices, which are like outposts of the IMPERIUM in every home, is so enormous that on the evening of that very day, as we're drinking TEA in the kitchen and talking about Phobos, the Martian moon that has an anomalous orbit, my hostess suddenly turns toward the RADIO: "No, I don't believe there's life on Mars. Those strange canals don't prove a thing. It's so far away, too, though its reddish coloration . . ."—she hesitates a second, then wags a finger at it, "Go ahead, you can put that opinion in my file!" And she flashes a smile for the RADIO and for the two of us, a smile that instantly dissolves into a shudder. Then at last I understand. We're "wired" like a police informant at a drug deal! An animal terror prevented people from disconnecting those RADIOS from the network that extended across the IMPERIUM: somewhere, in some remote panel watched by the Ministry of Truth, the red light for apartment five would start to blink.

That RADIO was on all day; in despair I tried to move it away from the foreground of my perception and into the deep background, to reduce it to a monotonous whisper, but then I would fall into the trap of the unforeseen silence, abandon my hiding place to look for it, and HA! It would hurl itself at my neck, pecking me with innumerable facts about the life and work of Vissarion Belinsky, the problematics of generational struggle in Turgenev's *House of the Gentry* . . . and so on *ad infinitum*.

The second day, I understood in astonishment that the RADIO was meant to be educational, a grandiose enlightenment crusade that haughtily ignored the laws of perception: several full-length lectures followed by two Puccini sonatas rescued from oblivion. I came to think that these RADIO programs had always been there in the air, guiding humanity through obscure centuries of ignorance, a notion derived from the joke about Popov, the scientist to whom Russians attribute the invention. When he tuned in his first RADIO, Popov was amazed to capture a transmission in the ether. It was Marconi, effusively congratulating him in Italian!

I have no desire to gain knowledge of the five different methods of hand milking practiced in Moldavia nor of the nineteenth-century infant mortality rate in Silesia. I left that house for good after the third day.

RASKOLNIKOV, INC. Saint Petersburg was still a good city for shuttered courtyards, dark stairways, tenacious drizzle, flooding, and usury. And old women who looked the part. Bent over, they dragged themselves along the treeless sidewalks, shuffling into hallways, collecting interest. I knew these were women who had survived the nine hundred days of the siege, but when I watched them go past I thought about Lizaveta the idiot, about money and the family heirlooms they may have preserved, wrapped in filthy calico handkerchiefs. Sometimes I would observe one of them as she made her way down the street, following her a short way behind. Suddenly her acute octogenarian ears would pick up the squelch of my shoe in a puddle and she would turn, and since, in her far-distant youth she, too, had read F.M., she would take a long look at the skirts of my overcoat and her eyes would be dry; she was prepared to confront the blow of the AX undaunted. In fact, these were all very poor old women but they still had faded TEA services or moth-chewed mink coats and hence lived in fear of a robbery.

But Saint Petersburg is still a good city for real usurers and antique dealers with collections of great value. Among the sources of this EN-CYCLOPEDIA I keep a clipping about the violent death of a collector of antiquities and his elderly female servant. I was seduced by the outline of the story: the elderly lover of Chinese bronzes and his housekeeper, and the thieves who put him to death.

There was enough there for several gangs: the collection was estimated to be worth almost a trillion rubles, or at least several hundred billion, that is, several tens of millions of dollars. An enormous quantity of money, enough to stage a live production of *War and Peace* with wounded Prince Andrei contemplating the sky and Bonaparte reviewing the troops at Austerlitz. The old man had amassed the valuable collection over years of intense smuggling that had brought him all those rubles. He could have organized a cycle of lectures on "How to make a million!" with no fear it would fail to sell out. The millions were in Chinese bronzes and antiques. Beneath tortoises with hieroglyphs on their shells, the whales of crepuscular Saint Petersburg swam, and above those tortoises stood the elephants of money-changing, the most basic form of usury, and there he was on top, the collector, crowning the whole mess, with the thieves beside him, about to cast him down into the abyss to swim with the whales. The reporter writes that the collection began with the contents of several containers smuggled out of the People's Republic of China, where the collector had traveled in the 1950s to build a hydroelectric dam. *Several containers.* Very twentieth century indeed. Those were serious calculations, revelatory of the character of an entire period. Sixty or seventy million Russians have died unnatural deaths so far this century: wars, hunger, and the Archipelago. This brings about a certain mental transformation. The man, the late collector, finds himself in China, and China turns out to be a very large country, and he thinks about shipping containers. The RASKOLNIKOVS who planned the robbery were also thinking about millions but not so many. That must have taken them by surprise. They load up with antiques worth many millions of rubles and leave the apartment. Then, after the crime is discovered, while the experts are cautiously making their way through hallways still replete with marble and bronze, the millions keep on disappearing. The *militsia* proceed to seal off the apartment, but the next morning they find the seals broken and several million more rubles of value gone missing. It would have taken four bands of RASKOLNIKOVS to ransack that treasure trove, and four F.M.s to describe the burns inflicted by lit cigarettes (they tortured him but he did not reveal where the cash was hidden) and the many AX blows dealt to both victims. There were too many millions there, and this is Saint Petersburg; the reporter makes no mention of any electronic alarm system or bodyguard to protect the antiquarian gentleman, or any policy taken out to insure against robbery (impossible in any case, since the collection was illegal). He describes only the vulnerable apartment, the knock at the door, the collector's glance out the peephole, and the tiny face of the elderly housekeeper returning from the market enclosed within it, the gilded frame of thugs who had been following her still invisible.

Do all of you out there understand? From here on, I'm expecting you to lend a bit more credence to what I'm telling you. Saint Petersburg was the right city for carrying out my plan. I'd rented a suite of rooms at the Astoria at a rate of $550 per night and I wanted to see the room F.M. had rented not far from there—I don't know how much he paid.

ROMANZAS. K** directed her questions through the mouth of her guitar and the succession of arpeggios gave true answers whose authenticity struck deep into the soul. At times, when night was far advanced, she would begin some ROMANZA of southern Russia, legs crossed: the wheat fields and the soldier who marches away with his troop. And there before us was a part of the world, a light region of the globe that was a field of undulating wheat and the women at their harvest in their calico shawls, some perfectly nineteenth-century province. K** would sing for hours in her slender thread of a voice, beautiful country ROMANZAS, and I would rest my ear against her flowered housecoat to listen as the cascade of *h*s she had stored up in her chest flowed forth. That was how we passed the nights, without electric light, without central heating. Is it true that we were still just the same as we had been for many centuries? To sing a ROMANZA and read tomes of Karamzín's *History* at night was better than switching on the RADIO. As we went to sleep, I would invariably say to her "*Que sueñes con los angelitos!*" ("May you dream of little angels!") which sounded like this in Russian: "*Pust tebe sniatsia angely!*" That certainly merited a ROMANZA, and I lost no time composing one.

Russian self-contemplation knows no bounds. When K** launched into one of those beautiful ROMANZAS with VERSES by Esenin, Tsvetaeva, and even Pushkin himself for lyrics, her eyes would sometimes fill with tears and she would interrupt the song to wonder aloud, "Are there other peoples whose souls are as sensitive, as highly strung and apt to resonate at the slightest breath of wind, as the Russian people?"

I would try to explain. I would pick up the guitar and sing *this* very beautiful song (one of the many that accompanied me throughout those years).

RUDI. The night before our trip to Nice we took a room in one of the YALTA hotels. At seven, as LINDA was dressing for her important stroll along the CATWALK (YALTA's little seafront promenade would serve the purpose), I dialed *room service,* still a novelty in the Grand Duchy's hotels. I asked for a bouquet of carnations for LINDA and stepped onto the balcony to contemplate the peak of Ai-Petri emerging from the clouds. Then, down below, alongside the garden's cypresses, I noticed a flower stand that hadn't registered during our arrival and resolved to go downstairs for the carnations myself.

I. The florist was listening to one of those horrible Muscovite ballads about scoundrels, pearly tears, apricot cheeks, black plums for eyes. (Each day spent in this country included hefty doses of this sort of vaudeville tune or gypsy dirge—from the Balkans or some such locale. No one turned his nose up at this lowbrow music and since the Russians were all very intelligent they always had a dazzling theory at the ready that could trip up even the cleverest objection; out would come the lecture about the inhuman suffering, the millions reposing in the Gulag. The long periods of time the intelligentsia spent in the work camps had forced them to imitate certain practices, and thus with honeyed voices they sang Гражданин начальник (Citizen Chief), which is how Aleksandr Isayevich (Solzhenitsyn) had once addressed his superior: *Graҙhdanin nachalnik,* will you allow me to make a suggestion? Already holding, hidden in his bosom, the bomb of the *Archipelago*.

Nervous about the many faces from the south I saw there and the possibility of thieves, I put my hand in my pocket and my eyes SCANNED fifty meters of street in both directions. An impulse transporting the information that a black form stood off to one side advanced devastatingly along my optic nerve as my fingers probed the soft leather of my wallet, but they were reached by the urgent countersign and remained there, grasping it tightly: someone very cunning was spying on me.

His face was straight off a "wanted" poster, complete with the perpetual struggle against a heavy growth of beard. I concluded that he was one of those picaresque characters from the south who are in the flower business and also dabble in thievery. He understood that I was waiting for him to leave before taking out my wallet and turned indignantly on his very high heels, crossing his arms like the bad guy in an operetta, mumbling insults. My eyes went off in search of some officer of the law to alert, but there was no one under the hotel canopy except the bored bellboy who—anything was possible in the Muscovy—might be in cahoots with the scoundrel from the south.

II. It was RUDI! How could I have taken so long to recognize him? The dark cloud I'd felt pursuing us since our arrival in Crimea took on form and density and acquired a face. I remembered the suggestion he himself had given me that night in the Astoria, his wet lips. "You should go south, to YALTA. Lots of casinos are opening there. The season has just begun." He'd mentioned this hotel in YALTA to me as a trap. RUDI realized that I'd recognized him, that his appearance on stage (the incarnation of the Baron de Charlus) had been premature, and that now he could no longer postpone the execution of the plan his carelessness had precipitated. Then he turned to me openly, smiled at me, and sent a signal to the crystalline lens of his eyeballs, which afforded me a glimpse of the sparkling metallic armature inside, the fearsome machinery.

III. It was RUDI! I spun on my heel, with a snap of the coattails of my *frac*. In the harbor, the steamboat that would take us to Nice let out an interminable blast and a band of seagulls suddenly veered out to the open sea. With RUDI and four of his men tearing after me, I dashed into the lobby, skating desperately along the polished floor, but at the magical chime of *do-mi-sol* the elevator doors opened and I saw LINDA about to step off, one pointy red pump already planted on the lobby floor. I slid another half meter, my face gaping at her, disfigured by a warning of danger I couldn't manage to voice. LINDA stopped short, astonished, and I threw myself inside, grabbing her as I fell, and, yes, did manage to activate the button—RUDI's eye, bloodshot with rage, glimpsed for an instant as the doors smoothly glided shut. Were we safe?

No. The doors reopen to reveal that we've landed in a dusty attic, a square of light shining down from a trapdoor, a climb onto the roof our only avenue of escape.

"Curses," I shout. "We shouldn't have trusted the LIFT!"

S

SAMOPAL (самопал). Due to a serious misunderstanding, Russia is reckoned a backward country and newspaper columnists calculate the number of years it lags behind the OCCIDENT. However, the IMPERIUM was not a country in the strict sense of the word; it was a land surveyor's polygon full of objects, artifacts, and replicas that were precarious, makeshift: самопал. The enormous grenade that aroused such terror in the OCCIDENT was no more than a stage prop, a dummy: *samopal*.

Like the imposter who arrives in a beach resort for the wealthy, steps out of a flashy PACKARD, and makes a show of his luxurious suitcases with their reinforced steel corners, Russia, in the assembly of nations, launched little rockets toward the ceiling, melted steel over the white tablecloth, and laid out railway lines from the salad plate to the punch bowl's ascending slope. Such manipulations provoked confusion and even an unconscious dread, as the prestidigitator of the moment inclined the billiard ball of his head to receive the bedazzled assembly's applause. (It's known that after one such function, in Berne, the Indonesian ambassador discovered a rabbit at his feet, chewing the edge of the tablecloth; when he tried to pick it up, its rubbery ears came off in his hand and the mother-of-pearl buttons rolled away, eye sockets empty.)

We lived surrounded by artifacts engineered for only the weakest pressures, mere appearance. In the buildings of the IMPERIUM, extremely inconvenient and unreliable LIFTS rose and fell, LIFTS that may have seemed old but were installed only yesterday. The IMPERIUM had everything it needed for a self-sufficient economy but all of it was shoddy in the extreme: the largest airline in the world, which was also the worst, the largest shoemaking industry and a considerable supply of individuals who might have been mistaken for barefoot Carmelites. It was a papier-mâché Utopia populated by unicorns manufactured in porous resin, light and graceful, but useless—yet in appearance nearly identical to the Japanese model from the last World's Fair, that could rear on its hind legs and gallop at top speed and would vanish if touched by a female nonvirgin.

The IMPERIUM was, in essence, a modern country, but of a parallel modernity, the greatest *installation* in history. *Socialist realism,* so myopically criticized, was in fact the greatest and most important avant-garde movement of the century, but it was a total art that left no gap between itself and reality: a complete model of a universe. Those OCCIDENTAL artists who fill twenty square meters of the Guggenheim with their "very daring" installations have never dreamed of working on this scale: one-sixth of the planet's area covered with mobiles, *ready-mades* and urinals, all *samopal*: the Universal Installation.

SCANNER. . . . *comme je passais seul devant le casino en rentrant à l'hôtel, j'eus la sensation d'être regardé par quelqu'un qui n'était pas loin de moi. Je tournai la tête et j'aperçus un homme d'une quarantaine d'années, très grand et assez gros, avec des moustaches très noires, et qui, tout en frappant nerveusement son pantalon avec une badine, fixait sur moi des yeux dilatés par l'attention. Il lança sur moi une suprême oeillade à la fois hardie, prudente, rapide et profonde, comme un dernier coup que l'on tire au moment de prendre la fuite, et après avoir regardé tout autour de lui, prenant soudain un air distrait et hautain, par un brusque revirement de toute sa personne il se tourna vers une affiche dans la lecture de laquelle il s'absorba, en fredonnant un air et en arrangeant la rose mousseuse qui pendait à sa boutonnière . . . Puis rejetant en arrière son chapeau et laissant voir une brosse coupée ras qui admettait cependant de chaque côté d'assez longues ailes de pigeon ondulées, il exhala le souffle bruyant des personnes qui ont non pas trop chaud mais le désir de montrer qu'elles ont trop chaud. J'eus l'idée d'un escroc d'hôtel qui, nous ayant peut-être déjà remarqués les jours précédents [LINDA et moi], et préparant quelque mauvais coup, venait de s'apercevoir que je l'avais surpris pendant qu'il m'épiait; pour me donner le change, peut-être cherchait-il seulement par sa nouvelle attitude à exprimer la distraction et le détachement, mais c'était avec une exagération si agressive que son but semblait au moins autant que de dissiper les soupçons que j'avais dû avoir, de venger une humiliation . . .*

Or: . . . as I walked alone past the casino toward the hotel I had the feeling that someone was watching me from nearby. I turned my head and perceived a man in his forties, very tall and fairly broad, with a very black mustache, who was lightly tapping his pants with a cane in a nervous gesture and focusing upon me a pair of eyes dilated by attention. He shot me a final glance, at once daring, prudent, fast, and deep, like a last shot fired off before taking flight and then, after surveying the area around himself, adopted a distracted and haughty air and with a sudden spin of his entire body turned to read a theater poster, absorbing himself in this task as he hummed a tune and adjusted the rose in his lapel . . . Then, pushing back his hat, thus exposing a brush cut that was very short but with undulating waves at the sides, he exhaled the sort of noisy sigh that is emitted not by those actually suffering from the heat but by those who wish to appear to be suffering from the heat.

It occurred to me that this might be a hotel burglar who, having noticed [LINDA and me], and decided to plot some strike against us, had just realized I'd caught him unawares as he was spying on me; perhaps he had adopted this new attitude of distraction and indifference merely in order to throw me off track, but his stance was so aggressively exaggerated that his aim, maore than to dissipate any suspicions he may have inspired in me, seemed to be to avenge some humiliation . . .

I. Allow me to explain. The ease with which, thanks to the SCANNER, I was able to reproduce fragments and even whole books from my library on my computer screen, caused my attitude toward them to change. Whether I pulled up some old fragment of my own work or a memorable passage from *A l'ombre des jeunes filles en fleur,* both seemed to emerge from the same nothingness and I came to see the beautiful text, too, as if I'd written it. Thanks to this innovation, the SCANNER, the pleasure of reading—*le plaisir du texte*—could be extended to the pleasure of writing and we could go along extracting excerpts from the endless continuum of books and construct a novel out of fragments of Tanizaki's *Captain Shigemoto's Mother* or Huysmans' *À Rebours,* or, if it was a matter of depicting a historical scene, a battle scene, a raw recruit's bewilderment among the deafening salvos, why not simply do a quick search and insert into my own text, word for word, the passage from *La chartreuse de Parme,* when Fabricio del Dongo stands on the bridge watching the dragoons go by: his perplexity? (Which was my own on the afternoon in YALTA when I ran into RUDI, prefigured by that of Marcel when he first observed the Baron de Charlus in Balbec.) Thanks to the SCANNER, which transformed the writing of texts into a game, making it *frivolous,* the writer can make use, without a twinge of conscience, of perfect, psychologically precise blocks of text that can even be numbered and cataloged for greater ease and velocity of access. We are freed from the laborious task of memorizing the few volumes we manage to read during a single lifetime and can make use of whole blocks of language that stand at the ready, entire warehouses of *axes suspended over the victim* (*The Idiot*, F.M.), *adulterous wives* in *shadowy rooms* (a section with a thousand titles) or that same adulterous wife in a *moving carriage* (*Madame Bovary*, Flaubert). To take the thousands of texts in the BIBLIOSPHERE and recast them into centos, without having our own authorship placed in any doubt. As Borges—I already mentioned him to you once—would say "*Lo tosco, lo bajamente policial, sería hablar de plagio.*" ("The crude and ignobly constabulary reaction would be to speak of plagiarism.")

SEA SIRENS. When I noticed an excellent pair of female legs I could never feel certain that some *Ivan* of my acquaintance would see them the same way. At times I was assailed by a vision of a pair of very long, almost perfect legs coming toward me, cutting through the air, precise as a barber's straight razor. Plunged into a trance by the rhythm of the heels, my eyes fixed on the silhouetted emptiness that, more even than the legs themselves, was those legs, I would hear someone beside me exclaim "Ай, какая русалочка!" ("*Ah, qué SIRENITA!*" or "Oh, what a little SIREN!") Frankly, hearing those words made me feel even more like a foreigner than Muscovy's eternal boiled stews! It was a line from a vaudeville show, the reaction of a blind man! The beauty of that woman had an exact physical meaning, and if in some Eastern European language she might be qualified as an "exquisite dish," in the Spanish I spoke, I would "*hincarle el diente,*" "*partirle el brazo*" ("sink my teeth into her," "break her arm")—and painfully.

I. The unknowable nature of the material world; the closed cycle of cultures that, like trees, rise to the heavens and die, side by side, without ever communicating anything of any importance to each other. This phenomenon came to obsess me in Muscovy, paralyzed as I was by the hieroglyphs of an alien and indecipherable life (the unfathomable original, there on the open page, that does not cease to trouble us as we read through its translation). For prior to our visit to Java, the imprecise breviaries we consult speak to us of the Javanese as beings very similar to *homo europaeus*. They communicate—we read—by means of sounds that, though guttural, are organized into an intelligible language. Credulous, we enter the verdant grove, book in hand, embark on friendships with one or another of the natives, and discover that we enjoy eating the grilled meat that is typical of the region. And since, indeed, we are able to establish that they, too, are men, that they have wives, that they suffer from deceit and disappointment and are sometimes overcome with hatred, we conclude that they are like us. We live on for two more years among the indigenes without giving the matter much further thought. One day—now more skilled in our use of their language—we come upon divergences in their very fiber, in the mechanisms of their being, divergences so horrific they leave us speechless. Then we rest our gaze upon a warrior: we watch him walk upright on his hind legs, we study his solid torso, his appearance that is, in the end, human, and we understand that the misunderstanding lies precisely there, in his deceptive appearance, because in reality these beings are as distant from us as beasts from another galaxy; they are other, they are not *men*. How could someone truly normal, *human*, exclaim, on seeing a lovely pair of human legs, *Ah, rusalochka ty moya!* I, who came from a planet where we not only spoke another language but also thought in a different way, would register these anomalies, so as to include them eventually in the true chronicle of this world I would one day write.

First refutation: These lyrics from a *guaracha*: *Es una bella mujer / con figura de SIRENA / y su hermosa piel morena / y cabellos largos hasta ahí. / Ay, yo no sé qué voy a hacer, / porque me tiene loco!* (She's a beauty, that one / body like a SIREN / that pretty chocolate skin /

that hair down to there. / Ay, don't know what I'm gonna do, / 'cause she's got me all wild.)

Second refutation: From *Entretiens sur les sciences secrètes* (vol. I, 1742 edition, p. 27): *Ecoutez donc jusqu'á la fin*—said the Comte de Gabalis—*& sachez que les mers & les fleuves sont habités de même que l'air: las anciens Sages ont nommé Ondiens ou Nymphes, cette espece de Peuples. Ils font peu de mâles, & les femmes y sont en grand nombre; leur beauté est extrême, & les filles des hommes n'ont rien de comparable.*

(Hear me out, and learn that the seas and rivers are inhabited, as well as the air. The ancient Sages called this race of people Undines or Nymphs. There are very few males among them but a great number of females; their beauty is extreme, and the daughters of men are not to be compared to them.)

SOSHA. Here's the story: I left the Jewish girl oozing juice (Henry Miller) and took off over the balcony, the rope ladder.

Before going to Russia, I knew nothing about Jews. I seem to recall that among the heterogeneous and indiscriminate mass of my high school classmates was a girl named Cohen but to be honest, I'd never heard of the Jews as a phenomenon worthy of particular attention. But no sooner had I arrived in the Grand Duchy of Muscovy in 198* than I fell headlong into the milieu of the world conspiracy. Half my professors were Jewish: a great danger. How could this have happened before the very eyes of so many Russians? The rector himself had a suspiciously Polish family name and . . . why hide it? He was a Jew through and through: the drooping lower lip, the hooked nose . . . My God, you could see it from a mile away! And what a surprise! That Cohen girl, my former schoolmate (of course she was), and the young geniuses at my Institute and that other violinist whose name . . . whose name . . . bah! Jewish, all of them! So by the time I met SOSHA (whose name was not Sosha, it's my feeling of guilt, my retrospective sorrow that christens her with a name borrowed from I. B. Singer: the eternally young, eternally ingenuous heroine), I was well prepared for the sad gazelle eyes, the luxuriant mane of hair, the purple lips of the Hebrew female.

And my God, she was a real talent. She made wonderful pen and ink sketches, she played the guitar magnificently, and she sang romanzas with a voice of velvet (we often sang duets together). At the age of eighteen she was a paragon of many virtues, and I felt powerfully attracted, beckoned by her perfume, still intact beneath its seal.

(Ah, but between me and that seal were interposed the *Protocols of the Elders of Zion*, the international conspiracy, the burning bush of suspicion!)

Her parents couldn't have been more kind. The stooped Jewish watchmaker who was her father, in fact, held an important chair at my Institute and her mother was a woman of dazzling beauty and a skilled kosher cook who imputed no religious significance whatsoever to what, in her mind, was the purely cultural rite of a family of cosmopolitan intellectuals, lovers of painting and good jazz.

"An intelligent woman with wonderful parents," easily classifiable and without any visible problem. Except for the hair. It was so abundant she couldn't find a way of tying it back that would keep its tendrils from escaping and she tried a thousand different styles without success. Though I never saw her in braids, which might have come undone all too easily, her hair flying in the wind once more.

The other serious problem (I'm almost forgetting) was the Gaza Strip, the Golan Heights, Tel Aviv, and, finally, the Grand Duchy of Muscovy, which was everyone's problem. The imperium was closed, sealed off like a tin can full of food, and there was no way out, no little key glued to the bottom or even, incredible as it may seem, any dynamite to blow it up with. We were all suffering there *kak sardiny v bochke* (like sardines in a barrel: Russia is an immense country, "like a barrel") and sitting at the piano her father sighed, and in the kitchen, kneading crackers without salt, her mother cursed.

Now, I—though only in half-measures, we might say—was a foreigner. Should the need arise, I could perfectly well go to the Kremlin, ask for the key, insert it into the lock, turn, and, click! рванут (vanish), with the enchanted princess wrapped up in a Persian carpet, the hair that might otherwise betray her sheared off as a precaution.

This perverse plot, hatched in the centers of international Zionism, was explained to me by my friend K**. "They're setting a trap for you," she warned. "Who has ever seen a Jew, of his own volition, hand his daughter over to a Gentile?"

(This is a long story, hard to tell, and sad.)

Indeed, I had received indications of an inalterably favorable disposition toward my person: prolonged discussions, the TEA grown cold, snow against the windowpanes. Rare volumes from the family library were loaned to me and during my visits the television was never switched on. I still have a pen and ink sketch of me done during one of those soirées. How can I doubt that she had fallen madly in love? The soft, amorous lines of that drawing are there to confirm it.

But why complicate things now, in memory? I had made several forays beneath SOSHA's skirt, stretched the elastic of her panties, breathed in her fresh scent . . . But though it was patently absurd, the information about the cruelty of the old Jews who had sacrificed millions of their own in Oświęcim in the deliberate aim of obtaining the territory of the State of Israel came to contaminate that scent. I thought I perceived, amid the vetiver and lavender of her white garments, other stronger aromas: that of calculation, malice, the dilated pupil glinting behind the monocle.

(Now there remains only the night of my rejection, that terrible night, the motor of this story.)

Sources: *Antiquities of the Jews,* Flavius Josephus.

SPITTING (see: EXPECTORATION).

STEPPE (see: ESTEPA).

SUMMA TECHNOLOGIAE. In Rotterdam, THELONIOUS visited a gaming arcade that led him to reflect on the possibility of a technological solution to karma, a mechanical portal to the state of pure pleasure. In short, the consummation of the entirely *frivolous* objective of human progress. To cross through the paradises imagined by Baudelaire without need of recourse to OPIUM.

This would achieve the goal of permanent well-being and crown the double helix of TECHNOLOGICAL development which, starting from the bottom, from the chill darkness of the cave, would appear in flashes that each marked the invention of a brilliant mechanical device, the blue and red nodules that sought to make our life more pleasurable: the spoon that could be used for scraping, a javelin in flight, Archimedes's screw, Fulton's piston . . . Achievements, it had now become clear, that were decidedly useless, that did no more than pave the way for the appearance of the SUMMA TECHNOLOGIAE, the fulfillment of what the Oriental mystics called the *alibi,* the creation of reality by means of an image. (Within just a few seconds THELONIOUS elaborates a complex cosmogony and seeks a final form for this idea of the world as the result of a game of Virtual Reality. A universe wherein the only discernible objectives—insubstantial, *frivolous*—would be to pair off into couples, accumulate wealth, enjoy good health and good humor, or what amounts to the same thing: to make your way through the labyrinth, find the seven keys, rescue the enchanted princess.)

I. *To Enter the Garden of Delights.* For now, in this Rotterdam arcade, we have to pass through the primitive and intermediary stage of helmets and goggles. Once a high degree of miniaturization of the devices—to the molecular level—has been achieved, we will be able to introduce the minuscule generator of visions into the cerebral tissue. Then our lives will consist exclusively of the unending melodrama of *the world I've always longed for.* Our visions will take on physical consistency so that when projected before us they float "as far as the eye can see," and as we're about to go around a corner, we'll know we will find another perfectly real street on the other side, with automobiles circulating and pedestrians hurrying past, which is to say that we'll know this same tableau will rise before us and that the end of that street will move away into infinity as we move forward, like the line of the horizon. (And isn't the line of the horizon the floating limit of a virtual field?) A game without locked doors or forbidden passageways. At the end of the staircase there will always be a room, and in it a bed, and on that bed, beneath an open window, the woman of our dreams. When, sated by these endless pleasures, we lose all notion of the falsity of this perfect world then we will never be able to leave, for we will entirely have forgotten the little doorway by which we came in.

II. *To Live in the Garden of Delights.* To walk naked through the Garden is to have no contact with this real world where you and I live. Therein is a paradise of vivid colors and simple forms, the pure and archetypal pleasures that in our earthly life we do no more than clumsily brush against. The concrete skin of an actual young woman is a mere imitation, an inexact copy of the cheeks of that same young woman as she exists in our thoughts. To live in the Garden is to cross over the abyss that divides these two from each other. (You, in the case of P.O.A., are not exactly the woman I desired, merely her *incarnation*.)

I could recognize the woman I dream of and even reproduce her in the camera obscura of my mind, which confirms my thesis. Each of us would end up elaborating his own private world and thousands of parallel worlds would come to exist, the worlds intuited by Saint Augustine. I imagine a multitude of Gods, all reclining in dark rooms and thinking of us. (THELONIOUS, RUDI, Kolia are no more than characters in a world created by me, a lone God.) And these parallel worlds cannot be reached or entered by others (the solitude of the Creator). Therefore:

a) The dreams where we see alien worlds are glimpses of the nearby presence of a neighboring God; they can be explained as a result of interference with the signal.

b) The multiplicity of worlds could also be explained as the tree diagram of someone who peoples his world with characters from fiction; the hair-raising and voracious Pac-Man, or the no less hair-raising bipedal models (men) who, when the moment arrives, sometimes generate other worlds, and so on into infinity. (All we can do is imagine the original form of that Creator of ours: either bipedal—"in the image and likeness"—or without any point of resemblance to his creations, the nebulous divinity of an unimaginable anteworld.)

c) In that latter case, we are, to him, creatures as horrible as the sanguinary entities who tirelessly pursue us through Pac-Man's virtual labyrinths.

III. *To Awaken in the Garden of Delights.* We've forgotten our former human existence and thus conclude that we have always lived in the Garden. One day, the serpent whispers the terrible truth in our ear; we break through the membrane, open the door, and discover our own nakedness.

When the veil is drawn back, we take those who control us from the center of the universe or the center of ourselves by surprise. (Isn't it amazing that we have such a peculiar vision of our own bodies? We see a hand covering a sheet of paper with irregular marks and our view of that image is blurred by a protuberance just beneath the eyes—which we call a nose. Aren't we concealed within this body? Isn't it true that we "inhabit it" and spy on the world through its eyes like Ulysses's men through the blind sockets of the Trojan horse?)

IV. *To be Cast Out of the Garden of Delights.* But every world has its real ending, like a program infected by a virus that will activate at 00:00 hours on Judgment Day. The Creator has allowed us to glimpse this truth, which presupposes an ending to our pleasant existence (the flaming sword) and the beginning of the anguished scientific quest (the iron balls Galileo threw down from the Leaning Tower of Pisa). Let us begin, then, to wander through a labyrinth overflowing with "pre-historic" skeletons that are nothing but the false evidence of a theory of spontaneous generation, the idea that we are the product of a simple confluence of natural factors. This fallacious "scientific" theory only manages to delay our arrival at the true solution, the SUMMA TECHNO-LOGIAE, for as long as the undoubtedly true hypothesis of an act of creation is refuted by the rigged proofs of a process of "evolution." The only merit of the scientific progress that ensues is to clarify the development of TECHNOLOGY and the arrival at the SUMMA: the belief in ghosts, the creation of reality by the image, the achievement of the *imagined* paradise. The return to the *Garden.*

T

TEA. An inexpensive infusion readily available to all, TEA enjoys great popularity across the IMPERIUM, where the practice of taking TEA with little cookies and homemade jam is widespread. The distinctly foreign climate required for the cultivation of TEA saved it from becoming a Siberian crop, "very much our own," along with the potato and the tomato which are both obviously and notoriously indigenous to Russia. The best TEA was imported from Ceylon in tins decorated with landscapes of verdant rolling hills. Bad TEA was perfidiously hacked atop the mountains of Georgia. Muscovy never had any particular problem with TEA, at least not during my stay in the country. Other less innocent infusions, characterized as delicacies (дэликатэссэн), were frowned upon for the aspersion of inefficiency they cast upon the IMPERIUM. For a period of five years, cocoa was entirely absent from the stores. The People's Comissariat organized a vast defamation campaign featuring a poster with these lines by G. K. Chesterton (translated into Russian, of course):

> *TEA, although an Oriental,*
> *Is a gentleman at least;*
> *Cocoa is a cad and coward,*
> *Cocoa is a vulgar beast.*

Followed by a brief text in boldface: "It is a well-known fact that as a boy Volodia Ulianov (LENIN) loved TEA. During his childhood in Simbirsk . . ." *et cetera.*

THELONIOUS MONK. As if I were called THELONIOUS MONK and she were LINDA EVANGELISTA.

I knew how to lead a false existence under those names; we had only to believe in our metamorphosis, leap onto the magic carpet of a perfect life, and contemplate from there the ciphers that denoted a bad year, any bad year—1990, 1991—as if it were 1819 or 1099 or some other historically significant combination of numerals, viewed from a distance.

Folded up inside THELONIOUS—a name that sounded like a Nordic mammal, followed by MONK, the dull thwack of its tail against the water—I was acquiring an incredible facility for generating limpid musical phrases, melodies that found their place in the teeming universe of songs that seem to have a natural life of their own, as if they'd been resonating through the air since the beginning of time. One such song had loaned me the necessary tone for this history. Two melodies that alternated throughout the composition: an initial one that came unstrung like a series of glass beads clinking against a rock crystal vase (perfectly reproducible with an arpeggio on the celesta), followed by another, pregnant with hope, that waited half a beat after the final *la* of the silver bell to break into the torrential whirl of a spring thaw: blue ice floes floating past, the cry of seagulls audible in the tune raised by the brass ensemble, the anguished lamentations of the English horn (the landscape, its Faustian distances).

That was the motif for the sunny, careless days. When I recount the genesis of this novel, my visit to the (CHINESE) PALACE, the music subsides into the graceful contours of a violin pizzicato, the sun and its shimmering reflection on the canals, the tender green of the gardens, a merry lightness that also serves as background to THELONIOUS's hopeful stroll along Nevsky Prospekt in search of LINDA. The crucial moment of recognition when the face of LA EVANGELISTA peers out from the features of a busker playing the FLUTE is signaled by a return of the initial phrase, which then takes flight, the opening of a window . . .

I. Let us conceive, therefore, of a very expensive book, product of an advanced TECHNOLOGY, whose pages are capable of determining what paragraph the reader's eyes will alight upon. Your stereo would simultaneously produce a certain melody, a central theme with its corresponding variations, written expressly for this novel. There might be other books, as well; that remains to be seen. We would have examples of LINDA's silvery voice, MONK's hoarse and melancholy laughter, cars racing through the streets of Saint Petersburg, the distant whisper of rain against the flagstones. (In fact, the computer software for this novel has been duly developed, and the interested reader can receive by return mail a CD with the *soundtrack* of P.O.A., its principal theme a continual bass line from which all other motifs ramify, restrained violins at moments of tension. It's called *The MONK*.) I visualize poor MONK fighting against a malady that, page after page, plunges him further into the unfathomable abyss of an excess of lucidity. A terrible thing. Lend me your ears: second introduction to *The MONK*.

MONK suffered from a strange malady.

U

ÚLTIMO VERANO DE KLINGSOR (KLINGSOR'S LAST SUMMER *or* KLINGSORS LETZTER SOMMER). Stripes of light fanned out over the sea, and there was a wind. When we stopped our PACKARD, LINDA kicked her feet over the edge of the door (the window was down), and jumped out onto the gravelly clifftop. Through the telescope mounted on the terrace of our DACHA, we had discovered mountain lilac in that small meadow across the bay. We had analyzed it minutely in the disturbing proximity granted by the telescope's prisms, and this cliff had seemed an ideal place to go and view lilacs. In my dossier I had located a military map of the littoral, a военная карта or *voennaya karta,* and studied various means of egress. We could get there by car, though my *karta* warned of a dangerous stretch of road. I showed it to LINDA: "the lovers' precipice," the name by which cartographers would henceforth label that anonymous spot in honor of our deaths.

LINDA wanted to bring Bovary's old lorgnette (she bought it in that antique store in Saint Petersburg), but I explained that we had to look at the lilacs with our naked eyes: the lenses would put too great a distance between pupil and meadow. "Anyway, tomorrow's going to be cloudy, you'll see."

And, in fact, we had only those stripes of light. LINDA went first, dreamily swaying along, our picnic basket dangling from her arm. That day, for the first time, she was wearing a new dress made of delicate pink ORGANDY, with a full skirt and ribbons lacing up in back. I've mentioned this already: I had the money, the time, the inclination, so why wouldn't I indulge myself with such an outing? Or rather, wasn't this expedition, to admire the lilacs the best of all possible day trips? I followed her, walking across the grass, my eyes on her nimble heels. For this special occasion I had selected a pair of Bermuda shorts with red and blue whales on a white background that represented the foamy sea. Each time I put one foot forward, I couldn't keep from glancing down at my thighs, covered by that fabric, which was simple but full of meaning for me. We had cut down on the ornamentation, streamlined the voluminous slashed pantaloons, eliminated the gold and freshwater pearls, but *conceptually* . . . were not my capacious movements a repetition of those of a Byzantine cardinal—the officiant's chasuble, the richly jeweled cross—proceeding toward the altar?

We sat down on the grass and I explained to LINDA that when the form of a flower—the silken petals, the stiffness of the stalk—emerges from the depths of chaos to exist for a certain number of hours and then decompose, we witness the consummation of an event that unveils a law, a norm. Beauty tends to appear in what is ephemeral, momentary; the brief life of the lepidoptera, the ice formations that a HARD FROST sketches across the windowpane . . . The monstrosity of a crag, a rocky outcrop—its formlessness—is perennial; it exists unaware of the vertigo of entropy or finds itself so far removed from it in time that entropy itself seems insignificant (the inhuman amount of time necessary for the friction of a piece of cloth to transform this crag's mass into fine sand). Extremely powerful forces exert their pressure from below on the magma of the material world and condition the emergence of perfect forms, casting them into certain preexisting reticulations capable of endowing these clots of energy with form. I believe in the existence of a unique crystal, a universal network that

156

holds within it the memory of the world; its discernment is anterior to our existence and as inexorable as the periodic table of the elements. I perceive two orders, one natural or divine and the other human. The natural goes about modeling a rose, a calendula, from the material it has at hand, and it is up to man, made of the same atoms and modeled within the same grid, to admire this beauty and confirm his own *identity* with the flower. True, there do exist differences in grain and resolution. A painstaking education, certain experiences, will diminish the margin of error and adjust your soul to respond to the slightest stimulus. Hence aesthetic pleasure is no more than an extremely precise and mathematical agreement between the vision of this flower and the model for it that we possess or perhaps—to make use of a more flexible schema—the model that can be created on the basis of leaves, petals, stem, and variations, though certainly within a narrow range of texture, degree of fuzziness, circumference, and consistency. And, as we go along, we adjust what we see to what we intuit or imagine. We should rejoice over this, rejoice that the good Lord has not tried out all variants, though I believe that he sometimes goes on intuition, that he, too, does not know *a ciencia cierta* (with scientific certainty) what the results will be.

LINDA: But in what way, then, does a change of time period influence taste? How does one explain a phenomenon such as fashion?

THELONIOUS: In the sense of an evolution or progress in taste? Not at all. The alphabet is very limited and not all combinations are possible or—and this amounts to the same thing—discernible by mankind. This limitation is the path of order, what saves us from madness. Our corporeal reality, our bipedal nature, introduces rigid invariables. God—the highest freedom—is therefore conceived as an entity without a body, not physical. And this incorporeal existence allows him to imagine all possible combinations of the universe. To us humans, he has allotted the few variations of the flower, the toga, jewelry, orders that permutate within a certain periodicity. A while ago I spoke to you of slashed pantaloons, the ingenious play of their multicolored billows of fabric, that feast for the eyes. Well, do you see that shadow, as if a cloud were passing over the meadow right now? Raise your eyes, I wanted to give you a surprise."

Over our heads, caught in the same air that surrounded the cliff, floated the striped mass of a Montgolfier. LINDA stared at it. For many seconds. The time it took for the long, segmented shadow of a rope ladder to extend down across her eyes, held wide in amazement. The final rung struck the ground with a dull thud. Someone, a celestial monster, the hot air balloon's crewman, was inviting us up into his basket. LINDA turned to me. The irruption of the great form of this balloon over the smooth canvas of our conversation had left her speechless. Finally she seemed to grasp it. "How is it that we didn't see it flying toward us? It came so suddenly, just like that!"

"It lifted off from the beach at the foot of the cliff," I answered, shouting up toward the basket, "It's all right, Kolia, I've got the cord."

Kolia had thrown down the anchor, which I managed to wedge between some rocks. The ladder swayed in my hands. I went up several steps and invited LINDA to follow. Once we were comfortably installed, I dislodged the anchor, opened the throttle on the gas and we rose into the air. "It's important to be able to invert one's point of view," I explained to LINDA. "A few moments ago we were seated down below, observing the perfection of the lilacs from the distance of our ocular globes. Now, suspended in this hot air balloon with its red and yellow stripes like the eyes of a deep-sea fish that allows itself to be pulled along by the ocean's currents, we can contemplate the meadow, appreciate how small that crag really is, see Kolia's black cap against the red patch of our PACKARD as he carries out my instructions to drive it back to our DACHA. So, then: what can we use this vision of the meadow dotted with flowers for? What ornament can it inspire in us?"

"For Christ's sake, IOSIF. They're just flowers!"

That time she was right.

V

VANILLA ICE. Motionless on the chair, with nothing in her stiffness to recall her former pliancy, LINDA presented her profile to me, the splendid colors of her face against the indigo of the sea. When she heard my question, she took a century to turn around and even then her eyes, as if imbued with all that blue, reluctantly followed the slightly less torpid movement of her head, lingering over the beach's pebbles, the gray mass of the breakwater, the white seagull perched on the café terrace, then sweeping the air over my head and finally locating me, as if with difficulty, resetting her gaze to zero, readjusting the beauty of the background to the immobile and insignificant figure of the writer.

"Some ice cream?"

She seemed to recall something, gave me a mischievous grin, and burst into speech: "As for ice cream—and I certainly hope you'll only order the kind that's made in those old-fashioned molds that come in every possible architectural form—whenever I eat one of those temples, churches, obelisks, or rocks, it's like a quaint geography I must take a moment to contemplate before transforming the monument of raspberry or vanilla into a refreshing coolness in my throat. My God, it wouldn't surprise me if you found Vendôme columns made of chocolate or raspberry ice cream at the Ritz, and then you'd need several of those, like votive columns or towers erected along an avenue in celebration of the glory of Coolness. They also have raspberry obelisks that rise here and there in the scorching desert of my thirst, whose pink granite will melt in the back of my mouth to slake me better than any oasis could . . . Those peaks of ice cream at the Ritz sometimes resemble the Monte Rosa, and sometimes, especially when they're lemon, I don't mind if they're not shaped like a monument but are as steep and irregular as a mountain painted by Elstir."

At last she had spoken. Her voice was still uncertain, but without a doubt she had now cast off her SIREN's tail. And she'd managed to surprise me with this disquisition extracted from the BIBLIOSPHERE. She knew I would appreciate the care with which she had selected it, the fact that it was by Proust, of whom I'd spoken so frequently. Immediately I remembered that one of KLIMT's redheaded models was called Albertine (like Proust's heroine). And delighted by the happy coincidence and because at that moment I saw the waiter approaching from the back of the café with our frozen concoctions, I shouted out in jubilation, "VANILLA ICE." (Which also happened to be the name of one of my favorite singers that year.)

The waiter was carrying the tray at a dangerous angle, though the glass dishes remained glued to its mirrored surface as if by some prodigy. I intuited that the inclination the waiter was imparting to the tray as he walked between the tables was inversely proportionate to the weight of the cups it bore, and that the waiter's brain was working like a well-oiled machine, in full mastery of his corporeal organization: the second-to-second disposition of his arm with the napkin draped over it, the suction pads of his right hand that gripped the tray so firmly, and his head which, a moment before the daring spin, announced the angle that both the tray and his torso would assume. Skills, wiles, acquired over years of intense rowing across the sea of clients, yet of which his waiter brain had not the slightest awareness. LINDA, to my astonishment, had given signs of possessing a more refined mechanism, capable of registering concepts, whole passages, such as the one she had just declaimed. I had tried to provide her with a guide to this apprenticeship, one of such logical force and powerful conviction that it would render the truth of *frivolity* irresistible, mathematically deducible, without need of any act of faith. Now I was ready to put her to the test, determine the degree of *humanity* that LINDA had achieved after three weeks of intense apprenticeship, attempt an operational definition of her intelligence (or *humanity*).

(In "Computing Machinery and Intelligence," A. M. Turing proposes the following:

[T]he "imitation game" . . . is played with three people, a man (A), a woman (B), and an interrogator (C) who may be of either sex. The interrogator stays in a room apart from the other two. The object of the game for the interrogator is to determine which of the other two is the man and which is the woman. It is A's object in the game to try and cause C to make the wrong identification. In order that tones of voice may not help the interrogator the answers should be written, or better still, typewritten. The ideal arrangement is to have a teleprinter communicating between the two rooms. The object of the game for the third player (B) is to help the interrogator. The best strategy for her is probably to give truthful answers. She can add such things as "I am the woman, don't listen to him!" to her answers, but it will avail nothing as the man can make similar remarks. We now ask the question, "What will happen when a machine takes the part of A in this game?" Will the interrogator decide wrongly as often when the game is played like this as he does when the game is played between a man and a woman? These questions replace our original, "Can machines think?"

I believe that in about fifty years' time it will be possible to program computers, with a storage capacity of about 109, to make them play the imitation game so well that an average interrogator will not have

more than 70 percent chance of making the right identification after
five minutes of questioning.

Which is to say: [This game] is played with three [participants], [the machine] (A), [a human] (B), and an interrogator (C) who may be of either sex. The interrogator stays in a room apart from the other two. The object of the game is for the interrogator to determine which of the other two is the [human] and which is the [machine]. . . . It is A's object in the game to try and cause C to make the wrong identification [so A, naturally, will answer without any kind of limitation]. . . . In order that tones of voice may not help the interrogator the answers should be written, or better still, typewritten. The ideal arrangement is to have a teleprinter communicating between the two rooms. [. . .] The best strategy for B is . . . to give truthful answers. . . . [If] an average interrogator will not have more than 70 percent chance of making the right identification after five minutes of questioning [most people will agree that the machine has demonstrated intelligent conduct].

Had she shed her SIREN's tail? How stable was she on her new legs? Was she ready for the CATWALK? Was it Anastasia or LINDA standing before me, her memory cells full of newly renovated information?

VASARI. The existence of important galleries of art in the Grand Duchy of Muscovy conditions the appearance of a certain sort of perfectly mimetic being: girls with an intellectual air about them, glasses, stockings that end above the knee, a slim portfolio clutched against the bosom as if replete with poetical compositions. During one whole summer I was intrigued by the frequent appearance of a woman beneath my window who would walk past with all the imposing presence of a condottiere depicted in oil paint. It took me two months to identify her as a fruit seller at a nearby bazaar, a coarse and ill-tempered creature. On another occasion I found myself in the cafeteria of a large research institution and noticed, among the members of the public present there alongside me, a gentleman with just the sort of precisely trimmed beard that is worn by a physicist who does top-secret research (atomic bombs, military lasers). The movement of his right hand through the air resolved all questions with academic exactitude, giving particular emphasis to certain phrases. I imagined: "The half-life of U-235 worries me," or "We must use the positron accelerator to bombard the nucleus with gamma particles." When I walked past him on my way out the door, I heard him confess the truth: "I'm telling you one more time: no yeast at all! None! A ten-liter demijohn, some cherries, and some sugar. That's it!" Later I often saw him in a neighboring bar tossing back glasses of cheap rosé, gripped with the firm hand of the lathe operator that he was.

I. The organizing eye. (In the *Confessions* of Saint Augustine [Book X], this important clarification:

Ad oculos enim proprie videre pertinet, utimur autem hoc verbo etiam in ceteris sensibus, cum eos ad cognoscendum intendimus. Neque enim dicimus, 'audi quid rutilet,' aut, 'olefac quam niteat,' aut, 'gusta quam splendeat,' aut, 'palpa quam fulgeat': videri enim dicuntur haec omnia. Dicimus autem non solum, 'vide quid luceat,' quod soli oculi sentire possunt, sed etiam, 'vide quid sonet,' 'vide quid oleat,' 'vide quid sapiat,' 'vide quam durum sit.' Ideoque generalis experientia sensuum concupiscentia (sicut dictum est) oculorum vocatur, quia videndi officium, in quo primatum oculi tenent, etiam ceteri sensus sibi de similitudine usurpant, cum aliquid cognitionis explorant.

For seeing belongeth properly to the eyes; yet we apply this word to the other senses also, when we exercise them in the search after

164

knowledge. For we do not say, "listen how it glows," "smell how it glistens," "taste how it shines," or "feel how it flashes," since all of these are said to be seen. And yet we say not only, "see how it shineth," which the eyes alone can perceive; but also, "see how it soundeth," "see how it smelleth," "see how it tasteth," "see how hard it is." And thus the general experience of the senses, as was said before, is termed "the lust of the eyes," because the function of seeing, wherein the eyes hold the preeminence, the other senses by way of similitude take possession of, whensoever they seek out any knowledge. —Translated by Edward Bouverie Pusey.)

II. I could never explain to myself the strange fascination that particular painting exerted on me, the strong attraction of the interlaced fingers, the languor of the powerful arms, captured in a relaxed and almost feminine pose. I'd discovered him at the end of the gallery, poised atop his lunar landscape like a rare species of lepidoptera, a gigantic Vanessa atalanta. His sadness, the blue marble of the landscape, those crystalline blooms, spoke to me of an ascent to a distant star: the exhausting journey, an extremely long effort rendered futile by the lunar desolation. They told me in the museum—or maybe I read it somewhere—that he represented a dejected or defeated demon. Was he the victor in full ascent or the victim of a fall? Unable to resolve the enigma I bought the best reproduction available—the one with dimensions closest to the original's immensity—and hung at the foot of my bed.

In the morning, as I emerged from long dreams, I would open my eyes in the room's semipenumbra and was invariably surprised by the presence of the *daemon* there. His coffee-colored torso and curling mane, the greens and blacks of that landscape, always posed the same question. Was this a lofty victory, though with no air to breathe in the void that surrounded him, or was he back on the earth, downcast, unable to break away from the pull of its formidable mass? One morning I leapt out of bed and without looking even once into his eyes went to the bathroom for my Solingen straight razor and resolved the question in the best way possible. The sad eyes, the weight of disgrace, the lunar despair—all that was rolled up and stowed away on top of the bookshelf. I cut out the bloom of octahedrons to his left and had it framed, a fragment of the most exquisite mineralogical exuberance. This painting, I decided, was far more suggestive than the other one, and for years, as I contemplated these unfathomable gems, entranced, I grew more convinced that this was the true and only contribution of Bruvel, the mad painter, to my formation: the *human* (in the old sense of *concern for the human*) was absolutely unnecessary. I was entirely wrong about this, I could not have been more wrong. As we shall see.

VIEW OF FALLING SNOW. It had been snowing since ten that morning. I asked the male nurse for a TEA and sipped it slowly without taking my eyes from the window, surrendering myself to the hypnotic power of the light snow that, agitated by the wind, seemed to ascend in inverse sequence, upward toward the distant floodgates of the heavens.

For the silence of this hospital room, for my legs encased in plaster, and for the depth of the sky, I had Prince Andrei Nikolayevich Bolkonsky, wounded at the Battle of Borodino: the unbearable splendor of our cosmic insignificance. The obvious existence of a baleful God who, with a single slash, had severed all the delicate threads of my story. Which of the two bodies touched the striped awning first? The small packet that was P.O.A. or my own eighty kilos of weight?

Downward: "A long way down since the time you had everything," which was another idea for a title, perhaps a more precise one. How long does it take a snowflake to fall from the sky? A month and a half? Two months?

When I awoke it had stopped snowing and I learned that I'd been here for sixty days. I also discovered a woman I did not know next to my bed. A young woman with hard features, her hair cut in layers at the back of the neck. It was LINDA. By now I could reach this type of conclusion very quickly. But her face was worked in shades of gray, as if bleached. Only the green of a pair of very expensive emerald earrings stood out, earrings I didn't recall having seen her wear before.

"They cut off my ponytail," I explained.

She turned to display her own bare nape.

I said, "I almost can't *see*, Anastasia. Because of the fall, apparently. I haven't suffered any attacks since I've been here. But why has it taken so long for you to come? Where have you been all this time?"

"I'm leaving, THELONIOUS."

"Dear God, no. Call me José, JOSEPH, if you want."

"*Well, I'm going to New York, JOSEPH.*"

"Speak Russian, Anastasia, for the love of God. Don't you understand? I was one step away from death. And what's more *olvídalo* (in the clear sense of *forget about that*). There's nothing in the OCCIDENT either. I'll explain this to you in detail if you like. A voice whispered in my ear and I heard it very clearly, as I'm hearing you now. I wept in rage, thinking about how to proceed with our journey, get more money. I was never that rich, I lied to you, all those stories about Chinese merchandise and chartered cargo ships . . . but a young boy's voice said to me, in a whisper 'A long way down since the time you had everything.' It was like being kicked in the head. It's a lengthier title than BREAD FOR THE MOUTH OF MY SOUL, but even more apt."

"No. I knew you were right when I saw you stretched out on the awning."

"But I didn't *see* anything as I was falling. I thought I would have time to study the trigonometric increment of the lines, but I didn't *see* anything. Only the final impact. That's what awaits us. I was impatient to tell you."

"That's ridiculous, THELONIOUS. What about *As I Lay Falling?* I could find two or three other good titles . . ." LINDA suddenly broke off and raised her palms to her temples.

"Are your temples throbbing?"

"Yes . . . No . . . Look . . ." she went on. "Aren't your striped pajamas the same pattern as the fabric of that awning? Weren't you trying to make me see precisely that sort of thing? As if when you fell . . ."

"My God, you're right! I hadn't noticed it."

". . . you became organically integrated into its pattern. Seeing you down there with your arms outstretched, like a starfish against the rippling seabed, I understood everything. It was a very eloquent ending. I thought you'd arranged it all. Even if you didn't, you should thank RUDI for it."

"But not New York, Nastia; at least Rotterdam."

(*But not New York, Nastia; at least Rotterdam.* Anastasia was making the same mistake as everyone else in Muscovy. A momentary and foreseeable error. There were many worlds within *frivolity.* I had tried to expand the perception she had of her beautiful little boots, to segment them into the fifteen lacquered nesting dolls of their softness, their texture, their pretty silver buckles, *et cetera,* although—I now saw with absolute clarity—it had been naive of me to anticipate that Anastasia would develop in that direction. In reality, she would never succeed in living in both worlds (that of heightened vision *and* that of the most sublime *frivolity*) with the requisite intensity or abandon. The boots she was wearing, so comfortable, polished with such great skill, did not touch her soul. She would never paddle happily in the sea where I'd moved with such ease. The time when I interrupted her dissertation on ice cream, shouting VANILLA ICE in jubilation—which was not the flavor that the waiter was bringing us but the joy I felt at being able to bring together, in my novel, the name of that rapper with a passage taken from Proust—she was left in a state of utmost incomprehension, and since I could provide no satisfactory clarification of the reasons for my happiness, she came to believe that I'd shouted VANILLA ICE because his music interested me as much as THELONIOUS's did and that these two artists' respective achievements allowed for some element of equivalence. I mean that it cost her a great deal of effort to discern what was present, what was rapidly taking place before her eyes, and though I had confidence that a woman of her talents would succeed in doing so at some point in the future, the most I could boast of, in the specific case of LINDA, was my success in making her adopt a lighter outlook on life, one that overlooked all the duties she'd always thought it necessary to carry out. You'll tell me that she was an atypical case, out of sync with the times, someone into whom the Doctrine and its central theses had sunk deep roots. Agreed. In essence, this was the cause of her current decision. She had come very far, though without undergoing any radical change. She'd suddenly begun to abhor her gray former life and was dreaming of a career as a model. She was going to New York.)

"Or wherever. To leave Russia."

"Kolia told me he'd like to go into the FOREST and never return. A day like today, with a HARD FROST, so that the snow covers his tracks. He's been talking about this all morning. He says he would lie down on a fallen cedar and let himself die of the cold, you know? Like those poor BRODIAGAS we saw in the south. He also told me that when people leave the north they carry the bodies of their dead away with them. The permaFROST keeps them intact."

"Wait," LINDA interrupted me, visibly upset. She stood up, almost knocking the chair over. "I'll bring you some water."

Five minutes later I heard a car engine roar to life beneath the window. It was true: she was going to New York. By way of good-bye she'd said, "Wait," clearly in the sense of my own summer sermons. I wept. I'm not ashamed to confess it. Tears rolled down my cheeks, uncontrollably. (Then, on the chair, I found a little bit of the LIGHT OF OTHER DAYS, the video of our fateful CATWALK.)

When we switched on the TV the next morning we learned of the fall of the IMPERIUM. I felt no emotion whatsoever. I merely noted that Mikhail Sergeyevich, the last emperor, had sent us a message that was full of meaning (apparently he, too, was in on the secret of FLUORIDE). The following is, undoubtedly, a fact of *general interest,* and I mention it here so that it may pass into history: *The last emperor met with a rock band (a very bad one, the Scorpions) hours before reading his resignation speech on television.* A most astute gesture on his part, no doubt.

In essence, this had been a time as old as any other. (Darius, king of the Persians; Chang Hua, the first Chinese ENCYCLOPEDIST; the Russian explorer Афанásий Никúтин [Afanasy Nikitin] who made the long journey to India in 1466.)

VERSE. In Russia they do write blank VERSE, as well, composed for declamation as a litany, the singular emotion of a monotonous buzz in the ears. Nevertheless, people on the street will acknowledge only what rhymes, and everyone knows long sequences of VERSE by heart. A young female trolley conductor whom I took back to my room one night with very clear intentions stood on the bed and declaimed the reasons for her refusal of me, which were taken from a long poem by Тютчев (Tyutchev). Dumbstruck, I desisted from my endeavor, for I could not oppose a woman who contained so much poetry. When at last, exhausted and out of breath (we'd ingested a good deal of AQUA VITAE), she went to the bathroom to take her clothes off, I already had another subject for an indispensible book: "Moscovy for Beginners." Declaiming long stanzas of rhyming VERSE is nothing, don't be impressed; it's a juggler's art, the same sort of popular erudition as a knowledge of many different dance steps would be for other more immediate peoples whose vision is less permeated by literary culture. Essentially, my trolley conductor, the nurse who took care of a friend, the gentleman who read me his deplorable VERSE for five full Metro stops, or the BRODIAGA I saw in an underground passageway trying out cadences and rhymes with movements of his head—when I asked him as I went by if he was writing VERSE, I turned out to be correct: he read me the one he'd just composed (heavy spikes of wheat, white birch trees) and offered to write me two salutatory stanzas at fifteen rubles per word—essentially, all these VERSIFIERS were, in the end, very elementary, uninformed, crude, whatever else you like.

VILLAGE (see: AGRICULTURE).

W

WHEN ME YOU FLY, I AM THE WINGS (SI HUYES DE MÍ YO SOY
LAS ALAS —EMERSON). Someone, a woman you met in a pension
in YALTA, an inconsequential summer romance, suddenly initiates a
correspondence and the very first letter leaves you disconcerted by her
refined mastery of the epistolary art.

In Russia, words retain a force that has been lost in the OCCIDENT.
I've received letters that could be published without the addition of a
single comma, and yet which I knew to have been written in a frenzy
of jealousy, in a single sitting, at a kitchen table amid pots of jam. A
kitchen I imagined perfectly: the house lost in the immensity of the
Grand Duchy of Muscovy, the point thousands of kilometers distant to
which her astral existence had displaced her and from where she was
sending me these letters like radiograms containing her coordinates,
the chronicle of her very dull life: the hated husband, the fearful gloom
of the world outside. The fortuitous intersection of our orbits in that
pension in YALTA had activated all her reserve systems—which had
been awaiting the signal of an embrace for years—and now she was
sending me detailed reports on all her functions: "You won't believe
me, but I haven't stopped thinking of you since that night we spent at
the lookout. My heart . . ." Nineteenth-century formulae that retain
all their power in Russian, a language well suited to descriptions of
delicate states of being such as nostalgia, the absence of a beloved, the
unbearable sorrow of a rupture. A system of categories that slammed
into me with the crushing force of a sudden crash to the ground after

slipping on a banana peel. In her letters I found fresh ideas, truths I myself had taken a very long time to discover, and her citations evinced an intimate mastery of such topics as music, sculpture, and the arts in general. (I'd had a friend, E**, who would sometimes speak to me in perfectly calibrated VERSE, stringing together miraculous improvisations on whatever it was she wanted to say to me at the moment: "Take the teapot from the fire, would you be so kind?" "Do me the favor of toasting up a slice of that nice bread!" and "Don't you agree we should make the most of the sunshine and go out for a stroll?" and so forth. To receive three perfect letters from this woman, letters I've kept all these years, barely surprised me at all, for it was clear that her breast harbored great quantities of literature in the rough. But the truly curious thing was that I'd also received admirably well-written letters from simple bookkeepers, nurses, attendants at child-care facilities. All of them exceptionally skilled at dashing off five handwritten pages, the complete naturalness of the epistolary novel, a genre I'd always thought of as rather too clever, somewhat forced.)

I'd picked up this letter at the porter's lodge as I was on my way out to an appointment. In the café, I asked K** to give me a second, tore open the envelope, and began reading. The woman described our visit to the lookout the evening before my departure and asked if I still loved her, if I remembered the starling chirping in the hedge that woke us in the morning. Her letter contained such tenderness, such promises of eternal fidelity, such certainty that I'd been desperately needed during the days since we'd last seen each other, that for a second I weighed the possibility of taking a plane, traveling 5,000 kilometers, and living with her for a while in her log cabin, lighting the woodstove in late afternoon, shoveling snow from the doorstep. Hurriedly I began my response on a paper napkin, "As you can see, I haven't even waited to get home before answering your letter." But when I raised my eyes to find the right word, the turn of phrase that would say precisely what I felt, I encountered the astonishment on K**'s face and my plan vanished in an instant. What sense would it make to travel so far when I have a woman right here within reach, *et cetera*?

WONDER, STEVIE: THE SECRET LIFE OF PLANTS. Through my capillaries ran the sap of a hundred thousand melodies, green globules that sometimes passed through the alkaline barrier of the cell walls and burst forth upon my lips in the form of song. Many of these particle-songs had names that were incapable today of reactivating the nervous centers of those intense sessions of listening—"BOOGIE SHOES," "THE SECRET LIFE OF PLANTS"—now more or less forgotten but that, during my adolescence, had been the key to deciphering the messages of truth we receive from the world's RADIO broadcast centers. At night, immobile in the penumbra of my room, I twirled the receiver's dial tirelessly until the galvanic discharge of *That's the way, oh-hoh, un-huh, I like it, oh-hoh, un-huh,* came pouring through, and I would shake my leg like a frog in an experiment, kicking out reflexively in response to the electric shock, and raise my head, eyes full of life. I should have explained all of this to LINDA.

I. In YALTA, we rented the DACHA of a former member of the Politburo, a small mansion next to the sea with a lovely little terrace for the sunsets. One afternoon, as I was relaxing on its warm tiles, an unforeseen sublimation occurred, the random union of certain molecular strings, and a clean and beautiful melody blazed forth in my mind. I hummed it twice without being able to believe my good fortune, leapt to my feet, and intoned an involuntary recitative, droning in a full and resonant voice—the voice of another man who lived in my bosom and spoke through my mouth—phrases that alluded to the beauty of the view, the warmth of summer, LINDA and myself. I was like an automat that had connected itself all on its own to the world centers of RADIO broadcasting and I laughed and apostrophized, emitting spine-tingling threnodies, ululating in diabolical tones. That was me, you must all believe me, singing out a sea of well-being.

This unexpected *rap*-ture awoke LINDA who came out to the terrace. "LINDA," I cried in jubilation, "I have the solution! To hell with P.O.A. Just one song! It's genius! It's fantastic! We'll sell a hundred thousand copies this year! Listen!"

LINDA heard me out for a long time without understanding. She didn't know a thing about jazz or Brazilian litany, or syncopation: her primary cultural stock consisted of long phrases performed on the oboe. Finally she slipped her verdict into a pause for breath: "Gregorian or plain chant."

I went on for five more stanzas before the light of that revelation stopped me short.

"Precisely. Gregorian chant. The beginning and the end. Do you think that's proof of an exhaustion of all forms? Great, perfect. Look, I know something about this, too." (I whistled the entire first movement of Vivaldi's concerto in E minor for bassoon and orchestra, impeccably.)

LINDA listened, flabbergasted. "Truly you astonish me. Wherever did you hear such good music?"

"But I told you about my CD collection. The best performers in the world: Horowitz, Kissin, Richter, almost all of them Russians (or *Jews,* whichever you like), though the point is not to linger over that. To go forward or . . . backward. Think of it: in one Handel concerto there are at least ten tunes that could be massive *hits.* When the violins attack the second movement"—I whistled it, inspired—"don't you hear a number one song on the *Billboard* top one hundred? This melody would be perfect for those VERSES by Blake:

The modest Rose puts forth a thorn,
The humble Sheep a threat'ning horn;
While the Lily white shall in love delight,
Nor a thorn nor a threat stain her beauty bright.

Then a block of energetic brass, blowing their hearts out . . . I have goose bumps! Two or three more repetitions of the chorus, then the song ends on a very high note and the brass cut off at one fell swoop. Nothing could be easier . . . No, LINDA, for the love of God! Those EURASIAN sonorities; I'd lose all my money. Bring me some lined paper, please. I'm tired of recording ballads I never manage to work through to my own satisfaction. Now that you're here and you know about music (though not precisely the kind required) . . . But listen: don't you hear? It's not a matter of the word that becomes music as it joins the rhythm, but the inverse process: the music coming undone into strips of words, the unconscious surfacing of strings of melody in their virgin state which, when intermingled and subjected to TECHNOLOGICAL processes, acquire the consistency of song. And we could add in that snatch of folk tune you were humming just now, that ROMANZA—why not?"

Y

YALTA. Sometimes I woke up to find myself possessed by the idea of boarding a plane and flying to YALTA. The irascible beauties I walked past every day in the Metro flowed south during the summer to toast their bodies in the sun, in a mood that could not be improved upon. A complete sampling of all that was on offer in the IMPERIUM— a world that extended from the luminous green of the subtropics to the white of the polar circle —deployed on deck chairs within a few meters of the sea. And me there, strolling along the shore, registering the astonishing diversity of EURASIA, which is to say, of much of the planet: pale blondes from the Baltic, Ukrainians with thick braids and honeyed skin, unsleeping Kazakhs, graceful Tartars; the daughters of hunters and reindeer herders who adorned their simple Taiwanese bathing suits with shamanistic trinkets and would often come down to the beach wearing slippers trimmed in otter skin: the cold breath of the tundra.

    I. YALTA is the nervously scribbled note, the sweet little foot. I knew women who, over the slow fire of a twilight on the beach—coarse sand inside their dresses—would isolate every fracture in an unhappy marriage, rubbing salt into the wounds of their lives. Late at night, I would hear the sighs and ayes that floated across the boulevards of YALTA and think of Ива́н Бу́нин (Ivan Bunin)—one of the sources for this entry—the writer who transported me to a new perception of the Russian language, which included "gentle breezes," damp petticoats, burning thighs. In the 1936 short story "The Caucasus" an officer arrives on the shore of the Black Sea, in search of his adulterous wife.

Он искал ее в Геленджике, в Гаграх, в Сочи. На другой день по приезде в Сочи, он купался утром в море, потом брился, надел чистое белье, белоснежный китель, позавтракал в своей гостинице на террасе ресторана, выпил бутылку шампанского, пил кофе с шартрезом, не спеша выкурил сигару. Возвратясь в свой номер, он лег на диван и выстрелил себе в виски из двух револьверов.

He looked for her in Gelendzhik, in Gagry, in Sochi. The day after he arrived in [YALTA], he went for a morning swim in the ocean, then shaved, changed his underwear, and donned a military jacket that was white as snow. At lunch on the terrace of the hotel restaurant he drank a full bottle of champagne, drained a cup of coffee laced with chartreuse, and unhurriedly smoked a cigar. Then he went back to his room, lay down on the sofa, and fired two pistols into his temples.

Z

ZIZI. In Paris, they called her ZIZI, short for Zinaida Pavlovna. She had been a lady-in-waiting to the Grand Duchess Maria Pavlovna, and in 1918 she fled straight from Tsarskoye Selo, the VILLAGE of the CZARS, to France. One limpid Monday in 1923, penniless, in despair, she went to a tryout for models at the haute couture salon of monsieur D**. The designer watched her move toward him, born along smoothly on those foreign legs of hers, gliding soundlessly as a swan: her grace, the fingers she extended in greeting as if they were alien things that did not belong to her. Monsieur D** dismissed all the little shop girls and seamstresses who had modeled for him until then. This was the start of another Russian period no less important than the one organized by Diaghilev years earlier. Understand? The exhaustion of trench warfare, gas creeping along the lowlands, the thrust of bayonets, the disaster of General Samsonov's defeat on the Prussian front, the famine that stalked Saint Petersburg during the winter of 1919; a tremendous effort of nature and the intersecting tensions of history, all were necessary, all were translated into the elegance of the former Russian nobility on the CATWALKS of Paris: fashion modeling transformed into an art. You could cause exactly the same furor today, LINDA, I imagine it perfectly. These Russian women, so strikingly beautiful; you, my angel, so perfectly in accord with my ideal of beauty . . . Russian beauty.

I. I notice ripples of light reflected on the canvas cloth beneath which I am slowly sipping a lemonade—YALTA, the sea, LINDA there beside me—and half-close my eyes. (At the next table, two Mongolian girls begin speaking in their harsh and unmistakable language, full of tongue clicks and hypnotically rolled *r*s. I follow that avalanche as the hare does the serpent's rattle. I know perfectly well that if chance had sent me off to live in captivity in Inner Mongolia I would eventually have kissed the hard lips of the younger one, would have tapped her white teeth with the nail of my index finger, untangled that hair, wiry as a horse's mane.) *Full of life, now, compact, visible* (Whitman). (*Lleno de vida hoy, compacto, visible.*) Me.

José Manuel Prieto was born in Havana in 1962. He lived in Russia for twelve years, has translated the works of Joseph Brodsky and Anna Akhmatova into Spanish, and has taught Russian history in Mexico City. He's the author of *Nocturnal Butterflies of the Russian Empire* and *Rex*. He currently teaches at Seton Hall University and lives in New York City.

Esther Allen teaches at Baruch College, City University of New York. She has translated a number of books from Spanish and French, including the Penguin Classics volume *José Martí: Selected Writings*, which she edited, annotated and translated. She has been a Fellow at the Cullman Center for Scholars and Writers at the New York Public Library, has twice been awarded Translation Fellowships by the National Endowment for the Arts, and has been decorated by the French government as a Chevalier de l'ordre des arts et des lettres.